The Immortal Universe

Vito Andrews

Matti Silver

eVw Press
www.evwpress.com
Email: publish@evwpress.com

ISBN: 978-0-9950351-6-4
First Edition
083117-15314BQBA

Cover illustration by Serene Lucyk of Shooting Star Press

Dedicated to Renée, who has endured more conversations about robots and science fiction than any patient partner should

&

To our immortal wondering brothers, those known and unknown, that all of us find our home in The Source we all emerged from and will all return to

Beginning of the End

The universe is dying.

It was the only thought going Slydin's ship as he sailed through the cosmos. The endless destruction and chaos he'd endured up until this point had led him to one, final desperate plea. He knew his destination wasn't going to give him the answers he needed, but he had run out of options a long time ago.

Death followed him, and he no longer knew what course of action to take to keep his crew safe. Given the situation, the death of the universe was the only thing he could focus on when a deafening buzz on the bridge erupted.

"Captain Slydin," a voice said, breaking him from his trance.

He blinked a few times and looked over in the direction of the interruption. It came from his first in command, Julianne. She hovered over him, her elongated ivory hands folded together to minimize the absurdity of their size, a trait she was always self-conscious of.

"Yes?" he asked.

"Does the Council know we won't be reporting in?" she

asked.

He looked up at her straight black hair, doing his best to avoid a direct gaze with her emerald green eyes. Gazing into them always forced an evoking of the truth, even when he didn't want to offer it up. He sensed she could always see right through him.

"The Council will want to know what the Elders suggest," he replied.

She slammed her hands down on the console in front of him.

"Damnit, Slydin," she whispered. "Are you disobeying orders?"

"They didn't give any orders," he said, turning his gaze from her. "How can I disobey a command that was never given?"

As if on cue, the alarms on the ship began clamoring intrusively to indicate a proximity alert. Julianne went back to her station and resumed her post while the rest of the crew went to work. Slydin kept his head down, staring into his console while thinking about whether he had made the right decision.

He didn't know what to do anymore.

"Captain," a high-pitched voice called out.

Slydin ignored the call and continued to stare downwards. He already knew how this was going to play out. He resigned himself to accepting his fate.

"Captain," the voice called out again.

"What is it, Mane?" Slydin called back.

"We're being targeted by a Federation ship. Military class. May I suggest—"

"No, you may not," Slydin interrupted. "Maintain course. We've given them no reason to fire upon us."

Mane looked back at his panel and began furiously tapping away at the translucent screens in front of him. He was the most annoying of Slydin's crew, but was the best communications officer any crew could hope to get. His idiosyncrasies and constant need to second guess everyone's actions always brought people to the brink of physical violence. Luckily for Mane, his skills were irreplaceable.

The sirens continued to blare and Slydin's console began to flash shades of red and amber. He stood up from his seat while continuing to look down at the warning being sent to his station. His ship was being targeted for destruction.

"Captain!" Julianne called out. "We need to hail them, now."

Slydin ran his fingers through his dark brown hair and stroked the back of his head. His eyes closed slightly as he stayed at his station pondering what to do. The alerts were now increasing in frequency, indicating the Federation ship's weapons were ready to fire.

"Captain!" Julianne implored.

Pressing a few buttons at his station, Slydin viewed the manifest of the ship that was currently ready to blast them into nothing. He knew he was in deep violation of the laws of the Council. Nobody went to the planet Javan unless they were given direct orders.

After a few swipes of the screen, the corners of his mouth turned upward.

"Keep our trajectory for Javan," he said, "and do not hail them."

The crew on the bridge looked towards each other, but said nothing. Mane went back to frantically working at his station, moving through screens at an increasing pace.

"Captain! They're firing!"

Before Slydin had a chance to respond, the bridge went dark, leaving only the eerie glow of the emergency monitors.

An electromagnetic pulse was meant to deliver one reaction: fear. A military ship with a clear target in their sight only disabled their enemy if they wanted to board and extract resources. The target ship would be useless to retaliate.

Slydin knew all of this, which is why he sat there with a grin on his face. Nobody could see it because of the darkness surrounding them, but it was there. Head down, eyes closed with a grin on his face. He knew what was going to happen next.

The rest of the crew could be heard shifting their weight and a few of them began to exhale after having held their breath the entire time. The sound of buzzing came through a moment later, overpowering all other noises.

"Captain, they are hailing— "

"I'm aware, Mane." Slydin interrupted. "I do understand how my own ship works and what an emergency communications signal sounds like. Don't respond until I give you the command."

Slydin stood up and shifted his head slightly upwards. Although the lights were powered down, there was enough glow from the nearby star to provide low level vision. Out of his peripherals, Slydin noticed Julianne walking over to him.

"What game are you playing?" she asked.

The buzzing sound increased in frequency.

"Captain—"

"I know," Slydin said before Mane had a chance to continue. "They really want to speak with me. Wait another moment."

"Are you willingly putting the lives of the crew in danger?" Julianne asked. "Is that what this has come down to? Throwing our lives away?"

He ignored her and counted the beats between each hail the Federation ship was sending. When the buzzing sound stopped, Slydin ordered Mane to respond. Within moments, a booming voice came through the communications system.

"Captain Slydin, you are on an unauthorized course and ignoring a Federation hail. Your actions are deemed worthy enough for us to board and commandeer your ship."

"Captain Jandin," Slydin replied cordially. Julianne huffed and stormed back to her station at the mention of his name.

"How would the Federation Council feel about you firing on another Federation ship without any signs of aggression?" Slydin asked. "You may be a military commander, but I'm an Ambassador. I think I'll win this one."

"You're the worst friend in the galaxy, do you know that?" replied Jandin sarcastically.

The smile on Slydin's face stretched even further. "You fired an EMP at my ship. Get me back online so I can be on my way."

There was a moment of silence.

"I can't let you go to Javan. No one visits the Elders without direct orders from The Council, you know that. Your rank as Captain might already be under deliberation for attempting it."

"I need to see the Elders. My Elder."

Another pause.

"You're desperate, aren't you?"

"I don't know what else to do and I don't think the Council does, either." Slydin dropped his head, allowing his mind to wander through the events of his recent past. He tried hard to stay in the present moment, although it was proving difficult

The ship's power came back online and a holo of Jandin immediately appeared in the middle of the bridge. Standing taller than Slydin, with a build larger than most of his race, he stared directly at the Captain who was still lost in his own thoughts.

"Slydin," Jandin said.

Slydin shifted his gaze toward his friend.

"There's a bigger issue," Jandin continued, "Javan's about to be attacked."

The Illusion of Control

The Ionian Elders of Javan were the reason the universe was held together. There's a strict sanction on visiting the planet unless specifically instructed for that very reason. Even a rebellion that was shaking the core of the idyllic structure of the Federation would know better than to attack, as their own existence depended on the Elders. Slydin relayed all this information to Jandin in hopes of him elaborating on his statement.

"I have no further details other than to protect the planet. It's fortunate you are the first ship I've encountered since my arrival. Unless, of course, you're the one who will be doing the attacking."

Slydin shook his head. "There's no time for humor. Who is planning the attack?"

"You already know that answer," Jandin shot back."

"Golates."

No sooner had the words left Slydin's mouth that his veins began to pulsate.

"I need to get on that planet."

"If you get on that planet, then both of us will be court

marshalled," Jandin replied. "Be reasonable, Slydin. Goaltes' forces don't have the firepower to fight against our military."

Slydin turned toward his pilot, Crimron, who was completely turned around and facing him during the entire conversation. The two of them shared a glance, which Crimron knew was a signal to be ready for an emergency command at a moment's notice. It was something the crew had practiced with Slydin many times, but never had to initiate. Regaining his composure, Slydin turned his attention back to the communication at hand.

"Captain Jandin," he said, his tone turning to a formality without any of the previous sarcasm. "There is a chance the Elders could pass along information which would be of benefit to the Federation. I would be happy to share it accordingly."

There was laughter on the other end.

"Captain Slydin, you're never going to change. You do know you're asking me to disobey my command, correct?"

"There was never an order to disobey. I am making my way out of my own volition and you are not at liberty to fire upon an ally ship."

"I will hold you accountable for anything that happens to me," Jandin replied.

"I would expect nothing less."

Slydin nodded towards Crimron and they continued course to Javan. The air among the crew felt lighter, as if everyone had breathed a collective sigh of relief.

. . . .

On board the Dehu, Captain Jandin turned off the holo and faced another right beside it. Standing in the ceremonial garb of a solid piece of purple fabric, wrapped several times around herself, was Shelah, the head of the Federation Council. She eyed him and nodded.

"Is the Jericho en route to Javan?" she asked.

Jandin nodded. "Yes, Slydin's on his way and promises to deliver information back to us if he should receive any. I don't foresee him stalling as he believed the part about the imminent attack on the planet."

"Captain Jandin," Shelah continued. "You know how critical this mission has become. The Ionians have not spoken to us in years and we are blind without their direction. You are to follow Captain Slydin down to Javan and get any information from him immediately, then relay it back to us."

"With all due respect, that is not what my post demands of me. What if there *is* an attack on the planet?"

"The Council has already sent several battleships to you. They will arrive shortly and defend the post. You have your orders, Captain Jandin."

Jandin nodded and the holo went offline. He stood there for a moment, staring at the empty space in front of him before turning his head up and addressing the rest of his crew.

"Our orders are to land on Javan. Turn on all cloaking systems and select a site within range of the Jericho. All communications are to be silent until further notice. Captain Slydin may not be expecting us to follow him, but his communications officer will detect the faintest signals."

He always detects everything, Jandin thought to himself.

"Listen up, crew," Slydin began. "Julianne and Mane will be my escorts while we are on the planet. I want the engines running hot and a constant scan of all frequencies while we're down there. The moment anybody even suspects we have a rogue ship within a parsec of this planet, I want to know."

The crew gave their affirmation and went to work as Julianne and Mane joined Slydin at his side.

"Captain, why are you taking me?" Mane asked.

Slydin motioned for him to follow as they made their way to the pod doors. They opened to reveal a pink sky overhead as a waft of warm air enveloped the crew's senses with an unearthly restfulness. Much of Slydin's anxiety slowly calmed as the light breeze relieved the pressure in his lungs, soothing him. Slydin closed his eyes and took in the moment.

Julianne inhaled deeply and then moved forward to lead them off of the ship. At the sound of her footsteps, Slydin opened his eyes and began to follow. However, Mane stood there, unable to move as he took in the scene before him. The two of them smiled at each other, understanding what this moment was bringing to their communications officer.

"Welcome to Javan, Mane," Julianne said. "Now let's get going."

Mane broke his trance and started after them. The ground was soft and each step they took felt like the earth was taking the impact. The fields of grass extended up to their hips, waving back and forth as if to welcome them. Slydin held his arms out, waving his hands over the blades to return the gesture, curling his fingers along a few strands, but never pulling them out.

"This place is…" Mane trailed off.

"Nothing like it in the universe," Slydin replied. "The Federation keeps a tight sanction on this planet to preserve it."

"It just feels welcoming. It feels like I'm home," Mane replied.

Julianne slowed her pace to match Slydin.

"I hope you know what you're doing," she said.

Slydin shrugged. "That's why we're here."

She bit her lip then gazed back towards Mane, who was following Slydin's lead by running his hands over the grass as well. His focus was anywhere but forward.

"Shouldn't you tell him what he's about to walk into?"

"It would be more fun if I didn't," Slydin smirked.

"Slydin…" Julianne urged.

He nodded and held his pace back to meet with Mane.

"What do you know about the Ionians?" he asked.

Mane looked startled at the question and shaking his head, he recalled the details that he knew.

"The Ionians are among the oldest races in the seventy nations. They exist as a whole in every aspect of life. The eldest of their people share their experience and knowledge with the youth through telepathy.

All the information from a lifetime is passed very quickly, disseminated and refined according to the needs of the generation. This race can predict patterns and even forestall future problems. The entire federation looks to them and sends vast amounts of information relating to medical, technological and environmental situations."

Slydin nodded his head, impressed but not surprised. For all his annoyances, Mane was formidable at his job.

"Correct. It was the Ionians who created and instituted the idea of a Federation of Nations that has developed and expanded to this day. When addressing one Ionian you are in effect addressing all of them and all those who came before."

Mane took it all in, gazing forward as he processed the information.

"Why did you bring me along with you?"

"You are my communications officer and while you can pinpoint any frequency in the universe, it seems, you have to experience a conversation with the Ionians. I want you to have that experience."

Mane looked touched. "Thank you, Captain."

"I also want you to keep in mind that they can read your thoughts and they don't always answer questions clearly."

"Captain?"

"The Ionians have taken part in every conflict our universe has faced and have been the main instruments in resolution. It's only now during our current times that Ionian Elders have been strangely silent about the existing crisis."

"In other words, they know why we're here and they might not tell us anything," Mane replied.

"Yes, so don't push your luck with them. We can't afford to have them go completely silent or the universe will be blind."

. . . .

"Captain, something isn't right."

Jandin went over to his communications officer and watched as she tapped away on her screen. He leaned in closely as several white flashes erupted, only to disappear.

Upon closer inspection, a few of those white flashes were followed by pale red dots.

"What am I looking at?" he asked.

"I thought I picked up a ping from the planet, which, as you know, is odd to begin with considering their lack of reliance on our systems. At first, I assumed it was our backup Federation ships arriving sooner than we thought."

"But?"

"Those signals are too weak to be coming from Federation ships. Instead, I decided to ping the planet."

"You mean you sent out a signal from this ship, directly disobeying my order?" Jandin seethed.

"One ping can be considered an anomaly. Nothing that can be traced back to us."

Jandin stood upright. "It can always be traced back to us. You better give me one good reason why I shouldn't relieve you of your duty right now."

"It's the result of the ping," she said, pointing at the screen. "After the ping diminished, there were a few flares of feedback."

Jandin leaned in once more as she replayed the results on her screen. She paused it when one of the white flashes dissipated and was replaced with a red dot.

"Right there," she said. "It's weak and cannot be distinguished, but it's responding to us."

"Are you sure it's not just the Ionians finally playing with some technology we gave them eons ago?" Jandin asked.

"No, Captain. Otherwise, the signal would be stronger and of Federation frequency."

"What are you suggesting?"

"Another group is already on the planet."

Mane's face dropped in disappointment.

"This… is it?" he asked.

Standing in front of the three was a dome shaped tent, with its wooden beams arching around a perimeter that could comfortably fit a handful of people. The fabric that draped over it was a thick cloth that had been dirtied by the passage of time, making it grey. Makeshift holes were cut in the top as windows into the outside world, allowing light into its folds.

"Welcome to the House of the Elders," Slydin announced.

Julianne smirked at the comment, taking an opportunity to watch Mane's reaction to it all. "Is it everything you expected?" she asked him.

"It's a tent in the middle of a field," Mane replied. "Why wouldn't they build something a bit more for themselves? Why wouldn't the Federation build something better?"

"What more do they need?" Slydin said. "All they really need is a meeting point and a few moments to communicate. It would seem wasteful to build anything more for such a short period."

The answer seemed to satisfy Mane, but his eyebrows

were still furrowed in confusion the sight of the place. They stepped up to the front flap of the tent, and Slydin held his hand up for them to stop. They waited a few moments before a hand began to peel back the entranceway.

"My dear Slydin, welcome back."

The hand continued to peel back the flap until it revealed a figure half the size of Slydin, but more than twice his age. The few whiskers on the top of his head and silver eyes that stretched across his face conflicted with his exuberant smile. With deftness, he slid out from behind the fabric and faced the three.

Slydin bowed his head slightly. "Trinome, it's good to see you."

Trinome nodded back and gazed over to Julianne. "Always a pleasure to see you as well, Julianne. I trust you've been keeping the ship together."

"I try," she said, grinning.

Slydin held his hand out towards Mane. "This is my communications officer…"

"Mane?" Trinome interrupted.

Mane nodded, his jaw clenched at the surprise of hearing his name without an introduction.

"Welcome to Javan."

"Thank you. I'm honoured to be here among all of you and to learn…"

"He does talk quite a bit, doesn't he?" Trinome asked, turning to the other two. Slydin bobbed his head up and down in agreement.

"Enough with the formalities, you're here to see the Elders. Or, in your case, one specific Elder, correct?"

Slydin nodded. "I am aware I have not been requested to be on this planet, but I have nowhere else to turn. There has been no instruction from the Council and our universe is being ripped apart by secessionists. We are seeking the wisdom of the Elders." Slydin paused. "I am seeking the wisdom of the Elders."

Trinome slumped his shoulders and hung his head.

"I know, but you are not going to find that wisdom here. Not anymore."

"Please, Trinome," Julianne interjected. "Can we dispense with the archaic posturing of language and get to the point? What's happened?"

"The Elders are gone."

Silence hung in the air at his comment. The wind blowing through the grass even seemed to stall, putting all of them in a complete state of bewilderment. Before Slydin could respond, Julianne reacted.

"Gone? How are they gone? They don't just disappear off the face of a planet."

Trinome stared right at her. "Yes, Julianne. They do."

After another pause, Slydin spoke up. "Why?"

"Elder Ronne still remains. He's been waiting for you and will explain what he can. He wanted me to prepare you for the conversation ahead. As you know, it won't last very long, timewise, and he will be making his leave after it's done."

Slydin straightened up and tore open the flap, storming inside the tent. Julianne followed, thanking Trinome on the way in. Mane nodded his head in thanks, still unsure about the conversation that just took place. He picked out enough to come to his own conclusions, but decided he would remain silent while they were inside.

That is a wise decision, a voice said in his head. He jumped at the voice and scanned the environment around him for the source. Trinome watched him and tilted his chin up, recognizing the experience.

"You'll get used to it," he said.

. . . .

"Council, this is Captain Jandin of the Dehu."

"Your orders were to be radio silent." Shelah stood there with her arms crossed in front and her head tilted slightly back.

"Yes, I understand. However, our initial analysis of the planet has shown there might be potential hostiles already. Requesting permission to perform a full sweep of the surface."

"Negative, Captain," Shelah replied. "Your analysis is either incorrect or showing signs of malfunction. Our best equipment is used to monitor the planet and we have detected no traffic to the planet aside from yourself and Captain Slydin. Now shut down communications until information has been gathered."

The holo went offline.

Jandin stood there, deliberating the options in his head. His fingers caressed his lips a few times while he burned a hole in the floor with his gaze. The rest of his crew focused on him, not daring to move. Shaking his head, he cleared his throat.

"Get the cruisers ready," he announced. "We're going to search for the source of the anomalies. If Golates is already on this planet, I want to be the one to surprise him."

"Captain," his first officer responded. "By doing this, we are directly disobeying the Federation. They could consider this an act of treason."

"There won't be a Federation left if an attack is already in progress," Jandin replied.

THE ANTICIPATED MOMENT

The cruisers rocketed through the sky at an altitude that was high enough to see the landscape without losing its details. Jandin took the lead, heading towards one of the three coordinates that his communications officer had identified as a source.

It was nicknamed the Lake of Fire as the water was a shade of red and encapsulated by a sandy beach around its perimeter. In its geographic location, it was also immune to heavy winds, making it an ideal place to visit all year round. It was a popular spot for the Ionians to just sit and contemplate.

As Jandin approached the lake, he took a moment to marvel at its beauty. It was not often he was permitted to be on the planet itself and he allowed himself the luxury of taking in the scenery. His attention then shifted to the surface itself.

"Any visuals?" he asked into the transmitter of his cockpit.

His two escorts were just behind him and they began to veer off to get a different angle of the area.

"Negative, Captain."

"Negative here, Captain."

Jandin felt something wrong with the scene beneath him. *Why isn't there anybody at the Lake?* he thought to himself.

"Circle in tight formation," he commanded.

. . . .

Captain Slydin. Welcome back.

The scratchy male voice stuck in all their heads as both Julianne and Slydin nodded towards its source. Mane was still getting his bearings inside the tent. In the middle of it was a formation of rocks in a circle with a hole in the center of it. Within the hole was water with steam coming off its surface, attacking the nostrils with the scent of the fresh grass they had just walked through.

Sitting on a wooden, three-legged stool in front of it was a robust figure dressed in a long black, cloak. His round stomach stuck out and it looked like it would put him off balance, but his legs were planted firmly on the ground. He sported a trimmed, white beard that seemed to compliment his crystal blue eyes.

There were no other stools in sight.

A pleasure to see you, Julianne. It's always nice to have the better of the two of you here as well.

A smile came across his face and the light-hearted tone resonated within their minds. Mane gripped his temples, not used to the mental invasion.

And this must be Mane. Stand closer to the water, it will help. Inhale deeply.

Mane stepped up and inhaled the fumes coming off the centerpiece. He suddenly felt at ease with everything happening. The new voice in his head felt comfortable, as if he was always meant to hear this way.

"Why haven't the Elders contacted us?" Slydin asked, cutting right to the point.

Elder Ronne didn't respond. Silence hung in the air and

Mane began to shift his weight from side to side, suddenly feeling awkward. Julianne noticed and she bent over to whisper in his ear.

"The longer an Elder takes to speak, the more important it is. They make you wait on purpose."

The waiting continued.

. . . .

Shelah carefully folded the purple fabric and placed it on the table in front of her. The satin touch of the fabric was a reminder of the delicacy of her position, but the colour was a constant reminder of her ability to lead. She was chosen by the Elders to lead the Federation Council and the consequence of every decision fell on her shoulders. Taking off the fabric felt like a huge weight was lifted from her.

A buzzing sound interrupted her thoughts. Someone was at her chambers.

Heading to the door, she pressed the viewscreen to see her visitor. The yellow armour of the Dodanim soldiers filled the screen. Their massive builds, as a result of their training since childhood, required uniforms made from custom materials to provide both flexibility and defense. Shelah never hesitated about allowing them near her as the loyalty of their race to the Federation was unmatched by any other.

She pressed the button and the aluminum doors slid open. Two guards were standing at attention, arms down by their sides.

"Your grace," the one on the right began.

"Please," she replied, putting up her hand. "You may address me as Shelah. We are outside Council chambers. Now what brings you here?"

"Vice-council Daoud requests your presence immediately. He says it's a matter of Federation security."

Shelah eyed the two for a moment, then tilted her chin

upwards, standing as tall as possible.

"Did he give you any other information? Is this just speculation?"

The two soldiers eyed each other, then returned their focus to her.

"He says he received word of a bomb planted within Federation headquarters."

Shelah didn't hesitate.

"Take me to him now."

Daoud received his intel from less than reputable sources and in some instances, although Shelah couldn't prove it, he would force it out of others. While they differed in their approach, they both agreed on the end goal — to keep the Federation united. If Daoud heard about it, there was no time to linger. Once again, she donned the weight of her office.

She just hoped it wouldn't be too late.

Although you will be tempted to interrupt me, you must allow me to finish. Understood?

Slydin and Julianne both stared at Mane, who shrugged.

I'm more concerned with you, Slydin, than your companion.

Now it was Slydin's turn to be taken aback.

The simple matter is there are no Elders left on the planet. I am the last one and agreed to stay here until our message could be conveyed to you. After what happened with Thoures, we knew you would be arriving shortly.

Slydin put up his arms and opened his mouth, but Elder Ronne continued before he had a chance to make a sound.

Through no fault of its own, the Federation is on the brink of collapse. While you may think it has something to do with the impending civil war between Golates and the Federation, the problem is much deeper.

Should the real problem continue to be ignored, there will be no legacy left and no ancestry for future generations to uphold. There will simply be nothing. The strengths of the nations that uphold the links between the worlds are slowly eroding them and they will not be able to save themselves of their own accord.

If the three were looking for helpful advice, their expressions gave away their disappointment. Mane dropped his head completely, eyeing the pool of water in front of him and wondering if now would be the time to stick his head in it.

The universe exists because we give it a story to exist within. However, if you can see the pages upon which this story is written, you will beg to learn more about the author and what has been written. This has been the journey of the Elders.

We have only been given a glimpse of the words, but those we read have taken us lifetimes to digest. Unfortunately, we too have reached the end of our capacity.

Slydin felt his mouth go dry. While the steam from the water continued to fill the tent, providing moisture against the skin, all he could taste was the bitterness of the words roving through his head. His mind began to shut down.

Slydin, your role is imperative to the continued existence of the nations of the Federation.

Slydin began tuning him out, not wanting to hear another word. He put his fingers to his eyes and rubbed them in circles while casting his thoughts in another direction.

Whether you choose to acknowledge me or ignore me, the message will still be delivered. You must travel to where the story still has strength. It is there you will meet the author and be given the key to the continued existence of the universe.

Julianne and Mane both looked at Elder Ronne with blank stares. Neither of them could make any sense of what he was saying.

Your frustration will do you no good. Listen with more than your head and be ready for my final instruction before I take my leave. Then, you must go.

The tent went quiet again. No more thoughts were looming in the minds of any of the three that were inside and Mane understood this to be a pause before another important point was to be made. He was going to ask aloud if he was right, but restrained himself.

The silence was broken by the sound of a blast in the distance.

. . . .

"What was that!?" Jandin yelled into his headset.

A plume of red smoke erupted from the edge of the lake, cascading upwards.

"Are there active geysers here?"

Three more eruptions sprung up in sequence after the first. The smoke was now billowing upwards, spreading across the water and land.

"It's cover!" Jandin yelled. "They're blasting smoke to cover their tracks. We won't be able to see anything in the air. Damnit!"

"Orders, Captain?"

"Back to the ship. We need to move by ground."

Jandin veered to the left, gripping the controls so tightly he could feel his hands struggling to keep their feeling. The physical sensations went to the wayside as his intuition came to life.

"Golates…"

. . . .

Shelah thanked the soldiers for their escort and asked to be left alone. They assured her they would be waiting nearby for when it was time to return to her chambers. Nodding, she turned her attention to the doorframe of vice-council Daoud. Like her own room, this was equipped with a seamless setup to prevent unauthorized access.

There was no way to tell where the door ended and where the wall began. Before she could reach her hand out to touch the buzzer that would gain his attention, a thin, white light appeared to reveal the hidden frame. He was waiting for her.

The smells of exotic foods wafted out as the door slid open and Shelah could almost taste the spicy dinner Daoud was enjoying in his room. The open door revealed a smaller figure, hunched over a table. He was wearing grey robes with long white stripes down the side.

His arms and feet were exposed, showing skin which was grey in both colour and attributes. He had lidless unblinking eyes and long stringy dark hair which gave him a ghoulish appearance. Daoud was a Scythian from the planet Magog. His race rarely displayed any emotions and their frigid looks only matched their callous behavior. It was this nation that housed the Federation prison system. Their villainous disposition created a perfect temperament for caging the greatest criminals in the system.

A large bowl was in front of his nose while he quickly shoveled the orange and green chunks of food within into his mouth. Shelah could taste the acidity from just inhaling the fumes it was giving off. If there was anything she would never understand, it was his appetite for unpalatable food.

"Step in and close the door behind you," Daoud said. He put down his eating utensil, which resembled a fork, but was made of glass instead of metal.

"You said there was a bomb."

He nodded his head. "I received intel a spy was planted here by Golates. The plan was to re-calibrate the reactor to set off a chain reaction."

"Do we know who it is?" Shelah asked.

"Yes."

Shelah's eyes lifted.

Daoud reached under the table and produced a pistol. He waved it at her and fired.

"What was that noise!?" Slydin called out.

Golates is here.

"What?" the three of them yelled in unison.

"How did you not tell us until now?" Slydin gritted.

I needed you to hear me first without the distraction of what was happening elsewhere. It is time for me to depart and for you as well.

"I can't leave now!" Slydin called back. "This planet is under attack and Golates is right outside."

He is not the answer to your problems, but he might be the springboard to the solution. Let him go and make your way to Peleg. Their citizens may be of help. The future of the Federation rests with you.

Before any of them could respond, Elder Ronne stood up from his stool and walked into the water. The steam seemed to swallow his being as it enveloped the elder, obstructing Slydin's view of his mentor. Shortly afterward, the vapour parted leaving only the Elders' black robe. The three stood there in silence for a moment, trying to process what had just happened. The sounds of more explosions rapidly brought their attentions back.

The flap of the tent opened and Trinome appeared.

"We need to leave," he said.

The moment he said it, Mane noticed that the smell of the tent had changed to the smoke of a fire.

"What's burning?" he asked.

"The planet," Trinome motioned.

The three of them left the tent and made their way back to the Jericho. Slydin signaled the crew to get the engines ready and to do a scan of the area. Whatever was happening, they wanted to be ready to fight back.

"Captain," the voice on the other end replied. "There's endless red smoke up in the atmosphere. We won't be able to see anything in the air. We're currently getting updated intel from Captain Jandin."

"What's Jandin doing here?" Julianne asked.

"It doesn't matter," Slydin replied, although he thought the same thing. "We'll need his help to take out the invaders."

. . . .

Jandin jumped into the surface rover, equipping himself with enough artillery to start a high-level offensive by himself. He didn't appreciate going into a fight blind and felt better being prepared for anything. The sleek black panel in front of him had few controls, as the rover was limited in its function. The glass encasing around him felt open, but also left him feeling vulnerable if it were breached.

The vehicle rumbled as the engines pulled against the force of gravity and hovered in place.

"Ride fast and keep a wide position!" he called out. "Our enemy is brutal, but not stupid."

A loud salute surrounded him. Jandin trusted his crew, but knew even they had to be plagued with uncertainty. Before setting out, he remembered that he should make one final call.

"Captain to Dehu, re-route a transmission call from here to the Council. We need backup and I need to speak with them immediately."

. . . .

In the Federation Council chambers, Shelah lay prone on her back. Daoud stood there, pistol still in his hand pointed towards her. Beads of sweat began dripping down his forehead and his heart was racing. His entire body felt numb, leaving him without a clue of how to proceed next.

The emergency override of his chamber doors springing open caused him to jump.

The Dodanim soldiers who had escorted Shelah took one look at the scene and sprang into action. The first one rolled along the floor towards Daoud, who instinctively pointed his pistol towards the incoming threat. Using the momentum, the soldier took off from the ground headfirst into Daoud's chest.

A spray of blood spurt out of Daoud's mouth. The pistol in his hand dropped to the floor with a resounding clang. He fell backwards and the soldier continued to move, putting one foot on his leg and the other on his chest.

The second soldier reached down and grabbed Shelah, picking her up and was about to throw her over his shoulder until he heard a grunt.

"No."

It was Shelah, whose eyes slowly opened.

"Put me down," she muttered.

Daoud started to hack, trying to say something, but the blood in his throat was causing him to choke. The Dodanim soldier maintained his grip, preventing even his fingers from twitching out of turn.

Shelah found her footing and shook her head from side to side. Tapping her left shoulder twice, a translucent blue screen faded from in front of her chest.

"The head of a council can never be too careful," she said. Turning to Daoud, she slowly shook her head once more. "As if I don't understand the danger of being the head of the Federation Council — especially during these times. Did you not get the briefing on advanced level armour?"

She walked over and picked up the pistol Daoud had used against her.

Muffled cries came from Daoud.

"Thank you for your service," Shelah nodded towards the soldiers. "It is because of your honour that we continue to stand as a Federation."

The soldiers nodded in response.

Before they could react, she put a bullet in the head of the soldier pinning down Daoud. Pivoting off her heel, she wheeled around and aimed for the second soldier who had tried to carry her away. He went to duck, but she adjusted accordingly and fired twice. He went limp on the ground.

Walking over to Daoud, she lowered herself to him and put the pistol right in his face.

"I don't know how you found out, but your secret dies with you."

She pulled the trigger.

On board the Jericho, Mane began frantically working their communications systems to get a direct line to Jandin.

"You're patched through, Captain!" he called out. "I also noticed Captain Jandin's ship has been pinging the planet for updated topography, which is an incredibly inefficient way of tracking movements—"

"Do something better," Slydin interrupted. "Don't tell me about it, just do it. Anything to help us out. Captain Jandin, what's happening?"

Their line was interrupted by static, but Jandin's voice eventually came through.

"We're tracking the situation on land," Jandin responded. "Slydin, you're no good in the air and you have no equipment to help us on land. Get off the planet! Get to the Council!"

"Negative. I'm here to support you in the hunt for Golates," Slydin replied.

"Then tell Mane to give us better intel on the planet. It's a smokescreen out here."

"He's working on it," Slydin replied. "Mane, where are we?"

"Splicing a connection to any communication signals on the planet," Mane called back.

"I need something now," Slydin commanded. "Captain Jandin, be careful out there."

"Affirmative," Jandin replied.

The communication ended and Slydin stood at his console, remaining still. Julianne came to him and stood shoulder to shoulder.

"He doesn't stand a chance out there," she said. "Not without re-enforcements."

"I know," Slydin said. "I just… don't know what else to do."

Julianne reached down to his console and brought up a few screens for him to see. Among them was the updated status of the Federation ships en-route to the planet. They were getting close, but wouldn't get there in time to meet Jandin on the battlefield. From a planetary perspective, they might have something to offer when they hit low orbit.

Another screen popped by, flashing a shade of orange. Slydin slammed his hand down to stop it from floating away and brought it to the forefront. He enhanced the message for himself and Julianne to witness.

Status Red

It was a message from Federation Council.

. . . .

Shelah wasn't sure how Daoud found out about her, but if he knew, others would as well. With three dead bodies in one room, it wouldn't take long before they realized what happened and whom to seek out for answers. She had to move fast if she was to make it to the reactor.

It was her dream to keep the Federation united and to mark them under a banner that would allow them the freedom to exist without conflict. She had grown up at the start of the secession of the planets and the rise of the civil war that ensued. At the onset of her career in politics, she decided it would be her mission to end the fighting.

That's why it came to such a surprise when Golates contacted her directly.

"You and I both want the same thing," he said.

"You wish to see yourself dead and your body floating aimlessly in space?" she retorted.

"We just want to be left alone and live in peace," he said, not acknowledging her disdain. "Each planet has the means to survive on its own. The only thing needed is a system of trade that is governed and nothing more."

There was a pause and before she could manage a response, he continued.

"None of the nations in the Federation are free. We all live under a forced caste system that *you* can undo? Are the ambassadors of each planet acting altruistically? Or are they just waiting to get what is theirs?"

As she escaped through the corridors of the lower level system, she still couldn't pinpoint what changed her mind during that conversation. What he was asking made sense in a way that only someone in her position would be able to see. This was a noble cause and the result would be the betterment of the Federation. This would allow the continued existence of all people for years to come — even if a few had to die along the way.

The end always justified the means.

The darkness enveloped her as the primitive lighting system took hold. The hallway disappeared, revealing illuminated marks on the floor to guide the way. No doubt they would be searching for her at this very moment. However, she knew the reactor was up ahead.

All she needed was a moment.

An Artificial Star

As Jandin hovered across the landscape blades of grass mixed with red smoke blocked his view. His targeting system was providing a more accurate readout of their trajectory, guiding them to the location where he presumed the enemy would be assembling. He kept his communications on high to hear for anything new. At a moment's notice, he would be ready to adjust his tactics accordingly.

The rest of his crew stayed close to him, waiting for his orders. They kept a lookout and felt the uneasiness of the mission press upon them.

"Keep a tight formation," Jandin commanded.

From his screen, he could see three of his crew surrounding him like a shield.

Slydin's voice cut-in. "Jandin, there's an issue at Council. They issued a status red."

"Why?"

"No details," came the response.

"That means it's serious," Jandin replied.

"Is Golates behind it?" Slydin asked.

"If you keep looking for his involvement in everything, you'll find him everywhere," Jandin shot back. "He's a tyrant, not a magician."

"I'm not convinced," Slydin returned. "Mane is sending you updated coordinates of all communications anomalies."

Immediately, the screen in front of Jandin shifted. The four white dotes indicating his crew shrunk and several dots appeared behind them. Without hesitation, he barked for his crew to turn around immediately.

. . . .

"Captain, we have a problem!" Mane called out. "They're behind Captain Jandin and heading toward us."

Slydin ran over to Mane's station and watched as he pulled up the latest efforts to triangulate both Jandin and Goltes. Several points were moving closer to him while the white dots representing Jandin's crew were moving further away, but starting to turn. Julianne was there a moment later to see the scene unfolding.

"What should we do?" Julianne asked. There was an urgency in her voice and Slydin felt his mind go blank. He didn't understand what he was looking at and his immediate response was denial.

"Are you sure that's correct?" Slydin asked.

"Slydin, make a decision," Julianne jumped in before Mane could answer.

The dots on the screen continued to move towards them. Slydin's fingers twitched as the scenarios played out in his head. Without realizing it, he blurted his thoughts out loud.

"Jandin is seeing this, which means he can probably catch up to them and…"

"Captain Jandin can only see the coordinates," Mane interrupted. "The red smoke makes visibility unlikely for him when they catch up."

"We have to leave," Julianne said.

Slydin's head turned in her direction and his eyes raised as if to ask if this was the only possibility. The crew on the bridge had all stopped focusing on their stations and were now paying attention to the ensuing conversation. While they were committed to the efforts in helping Jandin, it would require a quick, concerted effort to get off the ground in a hurry.

"I can't leave him behind," Slydin tried reasoning.

"Don't sacrifice us just because you don't know what to do," Julianne warned.

. . . .

Creating an artificial star amidst the Federation system had been the triumphant highlight of a united order. With the work of the planetary collective, each brought their own gifts to creating such a wonder. Not only had it become the triumph of the Federation, it was also used for their headquarters. It was a reminder of what could be accomplished if they all brought their strengths together.

Shelah stood outside the control room of the reactor core. This was the essence that powered the base and required unbelievably precise calculations and materials from every mining planet. The core worked by firing a high-powered laser at millions of mirrors, amplifying its power to focus on a single point. This single point of focus becomes the reactor, which then becomes a self-propagating power source. She was informed that if any of those mirrors are off even by a fraction, the core collapses in on itself.

Shelah wouldn't be able to adjust any of the mirrors. For security reasons, each mirror was bonded with a rare agent, mined from the deepest core of Pathros. Once set in place, the mirror would not move – even with an atomic explosion. However, she would be able to get access to the laser itself. If she could move it, the effect would be the same.

Exhaling, she punched in her access code and watched as the massive doors opened.

"Slydin, I'm telling you right now, take off and get out of here!"

Jandin was yelling into his headset, looking desperately for order in the chaos around him. Visibility had dropped to almost nothing and his squad was entirely dependent on the coordinates Mane was feeding them. While he appreciated having the Jericho and its crew's help, he didn't want that ship being taken over by Golates.

"I can't leave you here," was the reply. "Backup hasn't arrived yet and you need our help to find the enemy."

"We'll figure something out. Take-off!"

. . . .

Onboard the Jericho, the crew began to work at setting up a defensive perimeter. Given the uncertainty of the situation, and the inability of their captain to make a decision, they had to be prepared. Even if they took off right now, there was still a chance to be attacked on the way out.

"Captain, I agree with First Officer Julianne," Mane said.

"This situation is out of our control and fleeing would be the best option."

Slydin tuned him out. The suggestions of the rest of his crew became background noise as he fixated on something else at his station. While they were depending on him to guide them in this situation, he was still worried about the alert from the Federation base.

"Mane!" he called out. "Find out what the alert was about from the Federation and check to see how far the Federation backup ships are from here. They should've contacted us by now."

Mane nodded and went to work.

"Captain, should I fire the engines?"

The sound of Crimron's voice startled Slydin. It wasn't often his pilot spoke up during a critical situation as he was brilliant at anticipating the next step.

"Yes, be ready to fly, but do not move," Slydin replied.

The buzz of activity in the bridge raised the stress levels of everyone present. It was a combination of uncertainty of what they were facing mixed with a hopelessness at being unable to prepare for what was ahead. All they could do was wait and give themselves the best tactical advantage when the time came.

"Problem, Captain," Mane announced.

Slydin slouched his shoulders slightly. He wasn't ready to face another problem.

"What?" he snapped.

"I've been unable to contact any incoming Federation ships on any frequency. There is no response on even the basic subroutine that does ship-to-ship confirmation when in the vicinity of each other, which means…"

"Spit it out, Mane," Slydin jumped in.

Mane waited a moment before responding. "They were destroyed on the way here, or they were never coming."

Slydin froze, his face at an impasse. He couldn't feel any of his limbs, but felt in the pit of his stomach that his instincts were still on point.

"Mane find out about that alert, now!"

. . . .

As the doors moved, Shelah showed a certainty in her posture. Whatever doubts she carried with her were washed away at the crack of light pouring out from the door. There was nothing more to think about than what was ahead. This was going to be the defining moment for her and while she felt upset about not seeing how it would play out afterward, she was certain it would be for the better.

The doors opened enough for her to see in the room. Her heart stopped.

Lined up inside of the door, facing her, were an array of Dodanim soldiers. Standing shoulder to shoulder, they focused their attention towards her lone figure. There was nowhere for her to run.

"Daoud..." she whispered under her breath.

She felt stupid for not realizing he would've put safety measures in place in case something happened in the room. His paranoia was always too high to leave anything to chance and it finally worked in his favour. There would be no trial for her and no one to plead on her behalf. They were going to sentence her as a traitor and she would be executed — off the records.

Knowing she had nothing to lose, she reached into her shirt and pulled out a necklace with a pyramid shaped pendant on it. The Dodanim soldiers began to advance on her, marching in tight formation. Behind them, Shelah could see the alarm signal going off to indicate an emergency.

She ripped the pendant from her necklace, held it over her head and smashed it to the ground. Fire erupted and the walls began to shake.

Three high-pitched sounds erupted from the communications systems on board the Jericho. Slydin covered his ears at the sudden intrusion and felt as though he went deaf.

"Mane, what the—"

"Greetings, Captain Slydin."

Slydin shook his head and perked up at the voice. The blood in his veins ran hot and he could feel his breath leave him.

"Golates, what do you want?" he managed to say.

Laughter came over the system. It was a forced one, coming out in bursts through the mask he wore that allowed him to breathe. Slydin struggled to keep his composure as the taunting dragged on.

"This is how you greet me with all our history? The first thing I want is for you to be less predictable. The second thing I want is for the Federation to leave us alone. The second request should be fulfilled by now."

There was a pause as he waited for Slydin to reply to the comment. He didn't.

"I see my beautiful councilwoman has been delayed,"

Golates continued. "Or caught. It doesn't matter at this point. The Elders are gone and the Federation has been betrayed by its highest elected member. By now, you should realize we can get to anyone, anywhere in this system."

"I knew that warning was *you*." Slydin said.

Golates continued, ignoring the comment. "If your communications officer is relaying this conversation to Captain Jandin, tell him he shouldn't follow too quickly. We've placed mines along our path."

Mane looked over at Slydin, his face gone completely pale. Julianne stepped up to his workstation and began to manipulate the controls. Whatever she was trying to do, Slydin hoped it would help.

"Also, don't even think about trying to take-off," Golates warned. "We're familiar with Federation ship builds and will easily target your engine systems should you try."

"What do you want from me?" Slydin asked again.

"I want you to sweat a little bit," Golates replied. "There's nowhere for you to go and you are at my mercy. This is what our people have been feeling for ages now. However, I'll make you a deal: come out of your ship and surrender yourself and the rest of your crew will be allowed to leave."

"What's the catch?" Slydin asked. He knew Golates too well. He would want more than a simple exchange.

"I take over the Jericho."

. . . .

Jandin was indeed listening to the conversation as his team hurtled after Golates and his men. The words "We've placed mines along our path caused Jandin to call for a complete stop as he considered the next course of action. The red smoke Golates unleashed continued to block their view, which made it impossible to identify whether the threat was real. Every moment he spent out in the open was another opportunity for a surprise attack. His line of thinking might be paranoid, but he didn't know what kind of arsenal they were packing.

"Captain to Dehu," he called.

"Yes, Captain?" the voice replied.

"Get in the air and drop dummy packages on the field between us and the Jericho."

It was a long shot of a move as the Dehu wouldn't be able to see much from the air, relying on Mane's coordinates to guide them. However, his ship was equipped with non-lethal weaponry – warning shots. Dropping them on the field, Jandin hoped, would trigger any mines in the area and allow him to go through once more.

"Affirmative, Captain. Engineering has also come up with a way that we may be able to clear the smoke for you."

This was the best news Jandin heard since arriving on the planet.

"Whatever it is, do it now," he replied.

Jandin tuned back into the conversation that was happening between Golates and Slydin, just in time to hear the end of it.

"I take over the Jericho."

. . . .

The bodies of the Dodanim soldiers lay in a row.

Each one was smoldering from the explosion that instantly took their lives. The smell of burning flesh filled the air as the flames pierced through their armor and flared their skin. Smoke circulated through the hallway, carrying the destruction of the moment with it.

Standing in the middle of it all was Shelah. Her fingers dug into the inner canal of her ears as she tried to massage away the noise that damaged them. She choked at the smell of the burning flesh, feeling its contents deep within her throat.

Taking a moment to gain her composure, she eyed the damage around her.

A smile crept across her face.

The necklace with the pendant had been a gift she was given upon her appointment as leader of the Federation Council. It came from the people of Mizraim in the outer rim of the system. In exchange for never visiting them, they offered each head of council a useful memento of their planet, alongside updates of their research in energy technologies. It was the standard agreement each generation of councils received that no one dared to breach.

Shelah had modified hers in case a moment like this ever arrived. The effect was more powerful than she had expected, but she knew there were no more lifelines. The sounds of more soldiers running down the hallway let her know it was time to accomplish what she came here to do.

Stepping over the bodies of soldiers, she reached the control room where they monitored the reactor core. The displays that normally showed each detail of how the core was functioning were down from the blast she created. The room itself was still intact as it was built to withstand any act of destruction that might occur on the other side.

Tucked away in the corner of the room were a set of controls, two sticks emerging from the floor. The knobs on the ends were coloured a bright yellow. They were the manual override for the robotic arms on the other side of the wall, used only to perform the most minor of adjustments to the equipment.

It felt too easy for her. The Federation focused their line of defense on preventing those from landing on its base, putting each person coming through under the most in-depth scrutiny. Only after you had successfully passed the vetting process were you allowed to make your way here. Only two percent of all that applied for permission were ever admitted.

For the Federation, this was enough security. For Shelah, it was a fortunate oversight on their part.

Reaching out, she gripped the knobs and felt their warmth permeate her palms.

"She's in the room!" a voice bellowed.

Without hesitation, Shelah cranked the controls.

Julianne rushed over to Slydin and whispered into his ear.

"Backup is on its way. Mane and I re-routed a message through encrypted Federation frequencies. Keep stalling."

Slydin didn't want to stall. Standing there with no options before him, he began to hate this situation more with each passing moment. He hated not knowing what to do and he hated being cornered. Without thinking, he blurted out a counter-threat.

"You'll get my ship when you come aboard and take her from me," he announced.

"So be it," came the immediate response.

Slydin hammered down on the controls in front of him and the lights of the ship turned a bright green, indicating to the crew they were now in defensive mode. He pointed to Crimron.

"Get us up in the air at full throttle!"

"His threat…" Julianne warned.

"Evasive maneuvers on the way up," Slydin responded. "We can sustain the damage on the way out."

The ship shuddered as the crew got to work for. The system couldn't handle the smaller targets on a planet as it was designed for space combat, but Slydin trusted that the collateral damage caused would be enough to scare Golates off.

"We are a go in 3-2-1," Crimron announced. There was a tremor throughout the bridge as the Jericho began to work against the gravity of Javan.

"Sorry Jandin," Slydin muttered under his breath.

The gravity inside the ship suddenly lessened, giving everyone inside a momentarily feeling of weightlessness, then the ship came crashing to the ground. Falling over each other, it took a minute before Slydin could regain his balance while the ground beneath him continued to sway.

"What just happened!?"

Crimron tapped a few screens near his controls. "We lost power to the engines."

"How?" Slydin asked.

"We've had a hull breach," Mane piped in. "They followed through on their threat, Captain."

"Damnit! Everyone, equip yourselves accordingly. If they want to fight us, it's going to be on our terms."

The entire crew began arming themselves, strapping whatever weaponry they had carried with them on-board to their hips and back. Slydin grew concerned as many of them had never been in conflict. Intellectually preparing yourself and feeling confident to pull the trigger were two different modes of operating. Two different modes that even he'd had trouble working through.

Uncertainty followed their footsteps as they raced down the passageways to get into position. The plan was to lure Golates on-board using their knowledge of the ship's layout to their defensive advantage.

Blasts could be heard coming from outside, causing enough damage to vibrate the walls. They were trying to blast their way in.

"Shoot to kill," Slydin announced. "Those are your only

orders."

While he put on a brave face for the crew, he secretly hoped he wouldn't have to follow through on his own order.

. . . .

The smoke cleared in Jandin's field of vision.

Ahead of him, he could see several crystal balls of light scattered in the distance, gleaming from the sunlight that was miraculously making its way through the fog. Golates hadn't been bluffing. His army had planted mines to slow their pursuit.

"Avoid the mines and double down to the Jericho," Jandin commanded. "Dehu, provide support from above. See if you can get in touch with the bridge and have them take-off. The primary objective is to get the Jericho off the planet. Secondary objective is to take out Golates."

There was an affirmation from the rest of his crew as they sped off.

Come on Slydin, stand your ground.

. . . .

Being informed of what should happen and witnessing what transpires can sometimes be at opposite ends of a spectrum. Shelah felt this as she sat there, eyes closed, waiting for the Federation base to crumble around her.

Instead, voices from inside the room began to shout.

"She's here!"

"Take her out!"

She felt several strong sets of hands grab her by the shoulders and back, then felt the floor smack up against her face. A weight was pressed against her, giving her little room to breathe. Daring to open her eyes, all was shrouded in darkness broken only by the dull illumination of safety lights shining off the soldiers in the room.

"How long do we have?" one asked.

"Three days," came the reply. "Unless they can fix it before-hand."

Shelah suddenly realized she had been played as the universe's biggest fool. Her efforts to sabotage the Federation only resulted in a temporary setback. They would fix it, then they would put her on trial for treason. After her execution, they would begin to rip each other apart as the universe around them collapsed.

"I'm sorry, Slydin," she whispered.

The first blast to blow a hole in the wall of a ship is the most frightening. Afterwards, the anxiety levels just rise until the inevitable moment when enemies trespass into a space to instigate a war.

"I'm an ambassador, not a military commander," Slydin said out loud. "But I won't give him the satisfaction of thinking I'm weak."

Julianne listened to his outburst and responded in her own head that this level of self-talk would just make the rest of the crew nervous. She decided if Slydin were to continue musing out loud, potentially even talking himself out of engaging, she would have to take over. She hoped it wouldn't get to that point.

For all his annoyances, Mane looked to be holding it together beside the two of them. His hands were steadied on the simple pistol he carried with him.

Another charge was levied against the walls of the exit ramp. They didn't have to know the schematics to figure out where the invaders would breach. Crimron was the next person to speak up.

"Why haven't they surrounded us?" he asked.

"They want to take the ship intact," Julianne replied. Another blast came. "Well, mostly intact."

Slydin listened, but was still trying to figure out why they were easily able to breach the engine bay, but not the ramp the crew was guarding. His first assumption was that they only had one opportunity to use such a weapon that could penetrate the walls. However, there was something he couldn't quite get a grasp on bothering him.

"Crimron, what is the status of our engines? Has there been any report since we crashed down?" he asked.

"Captain," Julianne piped in. "We need to focus on the imminent threat."

Slydin ignored her. "What's the latest status?"

"Let me find out," Crimron said.

Crimron ran off to check on the crew in the engine bay, leaving the rest of them to wait.

"Mane, open a comm channel with Golates," Slydin commanded.

"Captain?"

"Don't question. Just do it."

Julianne hooked Slydin's arm and slammed him against the wall.

"What are you playing at?" she demanded.

He held a finger up and nodded to let her know the situation had come back under his control. Mane signaled to let him know the channel was live and that he was free to speak.

"Golates, give up. You can't get in."

A cackle came over air.

"My men haven't gotten to you yet? Give them another moment and you can tell me again how I can't get in."

Slydin looked back towards the ramp and noticed the blasting on the walls had stopped. That's when the sound of many boots marching against the floors perked his ears. He looked over in the direction where Crimron had ran and his heart sank. Several of Golates men were holding Crimron at gunpoint, forcing him to walk ahead as a hostage.

Slydin realized his mistake at once, they had come through the hole they created in the engine bay. The blasts were just a diversion.

. . . .

The Jericho came into view as Jandin sped towards it. In the distance, he could see many bodies surrounding its backside and a few who were grappling up the side of it. Billows of smoke were coming out from where they were climbing. At any moment, they would notice their approach.

"Spread formation and do not fire on hostiles unless they are clear of the Jericho," Jandin commanded. "Only direct hits and only leave your vehicle if necessary."

Right after giving the new orders, the Dehu buzzed.

"Captain Jandin, we have some news to share."

"This better be more important than taking out an attack on the Jericho."

"It's the Federation base," the voice from the crew responded. "There's been an attempt to sabotage it from one of its own council members. Someone who had been working directly with Golates."

"What!?" Jandin yelled. "Who?"

"They currently have the council member in custody, who was caught in the middle of the act. This person has also killed Daoud."

"Who is it!?"

There was a pause on the other hand, which Jandin understood to be hesitation.

"Tell me now or get off my ship."

"Head Council Shelah," the voice blurted out.

Jandin went blank for a moment.

"Slydin..." he whispered. The news struck him hard and

he wrestled with hearing it, but tried to focus on the next step that needed to happen. The Jericho was under attack and there was a strong chance that Golates would be the one to break the news to Slydin before he could get to him.

Jandin regained his composure and realized what the next step would have to be.

"Dehu, get Slydin off this planet and out of reach from any incoming Federation ships."

"Captain, is that the best course of action?"

Jandin didn't respond as he was too busy trying to make his way to his old friend.

. . . .

There was barely a trial.

The Dodanim soldiers who had captured her marched straight to the council chambers where life and death decisions were made. Small metal frames lined the outside of the room, circling the perimeter. It allowed each council member to see each other, while also being able to hear the testimony of any who would come to its centre.

They were short two council members in this emergency meeting. One was dead and the other was on trial. Shelah had no defense and she knew anything she said would be met with contempt and further their aim of executing her. If she kept her mouth shut, there was a chance she would survive for another day.

The first of the testimonies was from the soldiers who found her at the controls of the reactor. The second was from the security members who found the bodies of Daoud and the two Dodanim guards. They offered her a moment to say something in her defense, but it was worded in contempt.

"Have you anything to say for single-handedly destroying what we spent generations building together?"

Shelah refused to look at any of them; looking at the faces

of people she had served beside for many years and betrayed, was simply too difficult. They wouldn't understand what she was trying to achieve today. Not now, or ever.

Normally an Elder would be available to render the final verdict and affirm the decision of the council. However, word was given that no Elders would be present and in this situation, a unanimous decision bore the same equivalency.

It was unanimous that Shelah had committed treason and would be marooned on planet Ludim. It wasn't exile as much as it was a death by delivery. The planet could not support her biology and its people were direct allies with Golates.

Before they escorted her out, there was one final question: "Is Captain Slydin still on Javan?"

"Put down your weapons, open the doors and leave," the Plishtim soldier holding the gun to Crimron's head demanded.

Slydin and Julianne held their weapons at the incoming party, refusing to make a move. Slydin could feel the grip of his hands tighten and wondered if his aim would be good enough to take any of them out. At the rate his nerves were going, he wasn't sure it would be possible.

"Put down your weapons, open the doors and leave," the figure repeated.

Seeing Crimron in a helpless position tore at Slydin. As Captain, he assumed full responsibility for the lives of every person under his care; an oath he took seriously. He peered over at Julianne, who still had her aim on the attacker. Surrounding him were four others, each equipped with enough firepower to overwhelm anybody in their way. Even if one of them got the first shot, Slydin knew they didn't stand a chance.

He knelt and carefully put his weapon on the floor in front of him, maintaining eye contact the entire time. Standing back up, he walked over to the switch that would open the back door and reached out for it. There was a moment of hesitation, but he extended his finger and watched as the back doors opened and the ramp extend to the ground.

Waiting at the end of the ramp, with at least a dozen people around him, was Golates. His face was covered with a breathing mask, which had silver tubes extending from the mouth to his back. The maroon complexion of his skin could be seen in the area around his eyes and brow where there was no cover. His yellow hair was tied up in the centre of his head, accentuating the lifelessness of his greyed-out eyes.

He stepped on the ramp the moment it came out to him.

"A wise choice," he said. "Now secure this ship and get ready to counter Jandin. He's already blown our cover."

Golates approached Slydin as his people around him began to jog ahead.

"Captain Slydin, your services are no longer needed," he called out. "However, in honour of the service by you and your family, I will give you the freedom to walk off this ship a free man. I'm only making this offer once."

"You can take your offer and—"

Laser fire erupted.

Slydin dropped to the ground and watched as several shots were fired inside the ship. Golates men turned around and began to fire back, hugging the sides of the wall for cover.

"Close the doors!" Golates shouted.

Slydin sprawled out to grab his gun. Picking it up, he rolled over against the wall and took aim at those running toward him. He fired in rapid succession, blindly, not bothering to stop and consider the targets. A few dropped to the ground while others advanced towards him.

Julianne pulled the trigger and the figure holding Crimron fell to the floor. She had managed a head shot, where their protection was weakest. Crimron immediately took advantage of the situation to pry the gun from the fallen soldier's hand and fire upwards at the person directly beside him. Together, Julianne and Crimron faced their enemies.

Laser shots continued to fly in from outside the Jericho pinning Golates and his men to the walls.

"Push them back!" Slydin called out. "Put them in the crossfire!"

Laser blasts were firing from every direction and the only security of knowing one was still alive was the fact they were still firing. At the end of the ramp, one of Jandin's rovers came into view. Two crew members dressed in Federation colours climbed out from it and began to advance.

Slydin crawled back towards Julianne, who was on one knee and firing over him at Golates. A laser blast erupted beside her head, causing her to fall to the floor. Slydin wrapped his arm around her and pulled her close.

"Are you okay!?" he yelled.

"Keep firing," she replied.

That wasn't the answer to his question, but he kept firing at the ramp and watched Golates' men fall in quick succession. Golates had taken position behind the bodies of his soldiers and was firing back on Jandin's men who were coming towards him.

Slydin held his arm out and fired towards him. Sparks flew as he hit Golates in the arm, causing him to drop the weapon in his hand and hold his arm tightly to his body.

"Nice shot!" Julianne said.

He couldn't believe he made it and was thankful for the extra bit of luck that finally came his way. Another figure began to walk up the ramp and Slydin recognized him instantly. The figure marched over to where Golates had positioned himself, pulled out his rifle and fired it directly into his head.

Jandin's crew surrounded him and stood over the lifeless body in front of their leader. A moment of silence hung in the air as they looked upon the source of their trouble, now finished.

"Clean up the mess," Jandin called out.

Smoke billowed from the ship as the firefight settled. Slydin slowly got to his feet and walked over to greet his friend.

"Thank you," he managed to say.

Jandin put a hand on his shoulder. "Never open your gate to the enemy."

"I didn't know what else to do," Slydin defended. "They were going to kill my crew if I didn't let him on."

"Next time you stall, wait for me to get here. I had to make the choice between letting them take your ship and firing upon it, possibly killing your entire crew. I took the chance. We don't have time to discuss this further. You need to leave, now."

"What? Why?"

Jandin locked eye-contact with Slydin. "There's been a situation at Federation base. One of the council members has been exiled for treason."

Slydin felt the blood leave his face. "Who?"

Jandin paused.

"Your mother."

The air went dead.

Slydin couldn't stand as he processed what Jandin had just said. He felt his knees getting weak and almost fell to the floor. Jandin noticed him going off-balance and grabbed him by the shoulders.

"You need to get out of here, now," he told him.

"My m-m-mother?" Slydin stuttered.

"Yes. She killed Council member Daoud and then attempted to disrupt the core reactor. They caught her in the act. You need to leave."

Slydin couldn't think of anything else now except the loss of his mother. There were too many questions running through his mind to allow this conversation to end with him just leaving.

"Why? How can you be sure? *My* mother… She couldn't do anything like that… it can't be true?"

Jandin could see Mane and Julianne approach and nodded towards them. He furiously waved for them to move in. Mane went to one side while Julianne went to the other, each gripping him by the arm. Slydin fought against their touch, bringing his arms together.

"Captain," Mane began, "I'm sorry."

"Federation ships are on their way," Julianne followed. "Captain Jandin is right, we need to go."

Slydin shook his head. "Where am I going? What do they want from me?"

"Go somewhere safe," Jandin replied, taking his hands off Slydin's shoulders. "They're going to assume you're a collaborator and exile you, even if the evidence suggests otherwise. The Elders are gone, Golates is dead and the Federation is falling apart. This is the perfect time for someone to step up and make a play for power."

There was a pause. "You need to go, my friend."

"But the ship is damaged," Slydin fired back. "And what about you? And where will I go? Everyone will want my head."

"We'll go to Peleg," Julianne offered. "Elder Ronne told you they would be of help and the promise of an Elder is something we can still hold onto."

Slydin turned his head toward her, his voice filling with frustration. "How am I going to get there with a broken ship? Golates put a hole in my engine bay."

Julianne nodded towards Mane and Jandin, then pulled Slydin away from the two of them. She pinned him up against the connecting corridor and put all her weight into his chest. Her face went right up to his and she held it there for a moment.

"Listen," she said. "You are the Captain of this ship and the crew is looking for you to be the solid foundation. If you fall apart, then I need to stay strong. If both of us break, we all die and face a sentence worse than exile."

She let him go and walked back towards the other two. Slydin nodded his head slightly as he registered each of the words Julianne spoke to him. There was too much going on at once and it would only be a matter of time before his mind cracked. He could only hope that he would hit that point when the repercussions would be kept at a minimum.

The two returned to Jandin and Mane, who were deep in discussion. By the time they approached, they nodded towards each other and turned to include them.

"Your communications officer has an idea," Jandin said. "We put a temporary seal on the engine bay and use the Dehu to accelerate you to the jumpgate for Peleg. Before you can disagree with the plan, I've already called for a crew to begin the patch. We're working on a time crunch and we need to get you out."

"What happens to you?" Slydin asked. "They'll look at you with contempt for helping me out. Besides will a boost get us through the jumpgate without falling apart?"

"If we can pull enough acceleration from the Dehu," Mane began, "and the shields hold, we can make the gate. The sooner we can attempt it, the better and we're already losing time."

Slydin didn't appreciate being ordered by his First Officer and his Communications Officer, but he knew they were right. He also knew they were loyal and would never hold this against him. With Federation ships on their way, they wouldn't stand a chance of outrunning them.

"He's right," Jandin confirmed. "And I will do everything I can to hold them off. I'm still their best military leader."

He nodded towards all of them and made his way back to the bridge. The crew was already assembled and ready to go, waiting for further orders. Slydin took note of Crimron, who was at his seat and prepping the controls at his station. He was tuning out the attack that just happened and Slydin knew that he would have to approach him about it at some point.

Slydin gave the crew the orders for their immediate takeoff for the Pelegian jumpgate. With such an expansive system, and Peleg on its outer rim, the jumpgates were the fastest way of travelling between two points. Originally designed by the Pelegians themselves, they became the binding force of bringing all the planets together. However, even the ability to stay connected was falling apart. Like many others in the system, they were turning inwards and shutting themselves off from the rest of the Federation. The difference between their people and the rebellion led by Golates was the nature of how they did it, which was to provide the most basic of their technology to the Federation.

Slydin worried his presence on the planet would rile the Pelegians and force him to be turned away. If that happened, they would be marooned in the outer rim of the system without a hope of returning. If Federation ships were to follow them out there, it would make the situation a whole lot worse.

The planet of Peleg was another marvel in the system. Slydin couldn't help but admire the swirling silver and blue colours that covered the massive structure of the planet. It was one of the nicest places to visit, but very few did. To visit the Pelegians was an obvious ploy by those who needed something from them, making them always distrustful of visitors.

Their customs were known to Slydin, has been forced to study every group in the seventy-planet system. As an ambassador of the Federation, it would be embarrassing for him to show up and not understand the proper process for greeting, speaking and conducting one's self.

Slydin hoped it would be enough to allow him to land. The jump to this part of the system had taken a toll on his ship and the temporary seal put on the engine bay was barely holding. At best, they might be able to visit some of the other planets in the outer rim.

"Mane, please send a message to the planet. Let them know Ambassador Slydin of the Jericho requests an audience with the Pelegian Intelligence Academy regarding forward academic pursuits."

"Captain, should we really tell them—"

"Yes," Slydin interrupted. "Tell them exactly what I just said or I will hold you personally accountable if we become stranded."

Mane relayed the message and the entire bridge held their breath while they waited for a response. Slydin could see Mane furiously working at his station, potentially trying to catch any matter of communication from the planet. Although Mane could drive him up every wall in the system, he did appreciate the mastery of his position. If somebody sneezed on the planet near a transmitter, Mane would be able to pick it up.

"Captain, they are responding!" Mane called out.

"Are you going to put it over the comm?" Slydin asked.

"No, Captain. They are responding with instructions."

"Send those instructions to my station."

Slydin's station lit up with a detailed list for the Jericho to follow. While this would be a typical response for an uninvited guest instead of an Ambassador, Slydin was still breathing a sigh of relief. They were still allowing them to land on one of their sites and to continue the conversation in person.

"They are allowing us to land near their main research facility," Slydin announced. "When we land, Mane and Julianne will be with me to greet them and discuss our plans. Nobody is to leave the ship until I give the order. We are not going to instigate any form of action that could be construed as an act of aggression."

The landing field they were assigned was closer to the research facility than Slydin anticipated, which gave him hope they were willing to trust him. There were no further instructions on the way down, which allowed them time to appreciate the crystal blue waters on the way down.

Many legends surrounded the water on this planet, the most prominent being its ability to provide complete clarity of thought to whoever drinks it. However, even greater was its crystal colour and its supposed magical powers supposedly manufactured by the Pelegians themselves — a secret they had never confirmed.

Slydin readied himself at the exit of the ship with Julianne and Mane by his side. His mind began to circulate the entire gamut of ambassador protocols and to narrow down on the customs of the people on the planet. He didn't anticipate too much trouble because of their commonality.

"They are peaceful people," he said, letting his thoughts come out. "Let's show them the same."

The doors opened. Seven military guards were waiting on the platform. Each one had a plasma rifle aimed at the three of them.

"Oh, these must be the welcoming-committee peace rifles," Julianne replied.

Instinctively, Slydin held his arms up in surrender. The soldiers in front of him didn't flinch.

"Greetings," he announced. "I am unarmed."

They didn't respond.

A figure walked up to the platform and towards the three. It stood taller than the guards it was walking through and wore a white robe that just touched the ground. Its light blue skin shone on its elongated face. Its two arms were crossed in front as it approached.

"Captain Slydin," it said with a voice that resonated in octaves deeper than the ocean they were floating on. "You, First Officer Julianne and Communications Officer Mane can follow me. Please respect our security. We are on high alert."

"From what?" Slydin blurted out.

The figure eyed him for only a moment before turning its head.

"From you."

He began to move towards the connecting structure, causing the three to follow. Three of the military guards followed while the other four remained on the platform. Although slow, Slydin felt assured they were heading into the main research facility. It was a place he had visited on a few occasions during his first year as Ambassador to the Federation. He also knew he was the only Ambassador to visit them in many decades — a meeting the Elders of Javan put together.

He felt thankful at this moment for those visits and the Elders' intercession to make it happen. Slydin remained lost on those thoughts as they passed through a glass doorway and entered a brightly lit hallway. Endless lights filled the corridor, each one set to a different brightness. Together, they helped to simulate a nature walk to give the researchers a feeling of happiness when they left their rooms.

Mane couldn't contain himself.

"This is amazing!"

Slydin nudged him. "Quiet, Mane. Remember what I told you about us being marooned."

Mane pursed his lips at the thought and continued on without saying a word.

The figure took them into a room encased with glass walls. Behind the walls were swirling ocean currents that mimicked the waters they were currently on. The mirage was brilliant enough to not allow anybody to see out of the room while making those inside feel calm.

"I'll be back," the figure said.

He disappeared and closed the door behind him, leaving the three inside the empty space.

"Why is this room empty?" Julianne asked. "This doesn't seem right."

Slydin thought about it for a moment and remembered a detail from his early visits.

"This is a meeting room," he replied. "The Pelegians don't sit for meetings, for work or for any formal engagements. The rumour is their constant standing is why they're so tall."

He hoped his joke would help lighten the mood, but the other two looked clearly uncomfortable. The door opened and three figures walked in. They marched to the opposite end of the room and stood against the wall. Immediately, the view of the ocean changed into a completley black canvas.

"Welcome back to Peleg, Ambassador Slydin."

"Thank you, Ambassador Yirhan." Slydin replied. "And please forgive my outburst moments earlier. We've been on edge and were concerned we weren't going to make it here."

"We know," Yirhan replied. "This meeting needs to be brief and to the point. Afterwards, we will offer whatever we can to your ship and your crew and then you can be off again."

"Off to where?" Julianne jumped in.

The Pelegians exchanged glances.

"To find the special point in the universe," Yirhan answered.

Now the three crew members exchanged glances, unsure of what was just said.

"Perhaps this meeting won't be so brief. Let's begin this meeting with a step back from where we planned. You're here because the universe is about to end."

An Extended Meeting

If there was any way to start a meeting to get everyone's attention, Yirhan had just mastered it. Mane and Julianne stood there with their mouths hung open.

"Pragmatically," Yirhan continued, "you arrived here because you had nowhere else to turn after the betrayal of your mother."

Slydin cringed at the reminder.

"Or perhaps we're all here for a reason… aside from the reason of making stupid decisions." Yirhan adjusted his robe and stretched out his arms to both sides. "To my left is Buerna and to my right is Arwa. These two are the planet's foremost experts in the field of precision calculations. They are here to answer any questions after I brief you and to elaborate on anything I may miss."

Immediately behind them, the screen illuminated an image of a silver loop.

"What you're viewing is the evolution of the jump gate. Our descendants, the mathematical geniuses of Arphaxad, took the early design and found a way to program them for higher precision throughout the system."

"This iteration would allow citizens of one planet to pass through and visit another planet. Of course, the Federation would never fund a project of this scope, especially with the weak stability that is pervading the system. Given our limited resources, we did manage to make it work on our planet. We tested it here before attempting to bring it to the other planets."

"Why wouldn't the Federation want to develop this or at the very least, take the prototype and get their own team working on it?" Slydin asked.

"Two questions," Mane piped in. "Did you have a greater energy source for further distances and how close did you get on this planet?"

"We succeeded on this planet..."

There was total silence until Yirhan continued in a subdued voice.

Arwa jumped in. Yirhan and Buerna stepped away as she began to speak.

"This is where your limitations of how jump gates work prevent you from seeing the full technological implications of what we created."

She began to manipulate her fingers along the wall behind her until the loop showed a series of calculations surrounding it.

"The jump gates require a point on each end to ensure the continuation of energy and stabilization of a gateway tunnel. The portals we created only require an entry point and could be programmed to exit the subject anywhere else. To give an example, I could build one here and program it to send me in the middle of the Federation base."

Julianne spoke up. "Why haven't you shared this with anyone else?"

Arwa stepped back and Yirhan came to the forefront once more.

"The issue with the portals is the energy requirement, especially in instances of greater distance. Given our resources on this planet, our energy requirements only allowed for short distances and we wanted to ensure it worked before sharing the result with others."

"Then it all went wrong. At first, our subjects would end up slightly off from the calculations we programmed. Then the errors in distance began to increase and before long, there were reports of our subjects ending up in the upper atmosphere. Had we not shut them down at that point, we're certain they would have ended up in the vastness of space."

"After further assessment, we determined the problem extended beyond our portal calculations. Our entire system would now be at the mercy of all those leaving it, which in turn would cause mass chaos. There is no blame to be put on any one race, or planet. It is a problem without a solution."

"You obviously have a solution if you allowed us to land," Slydin replied. "And what does this have to do with the universe dying?"

"It was simply a matter of time before the planets went to war with each other," Yirhan responded. "The situation on the Federation base only accelerated what was bound to happen. Based on our stringent observations and calculations, the laws holding this universe together are falling apart and this is being reflected in the behaviour of our system."

"We don't like to provide solutions that aren't mathematically calculated to perfection. However, Elder Ronne asked us to accept you on this planet to attempt a resolution that would require, what he called, a leap of faith."

"What does that mean?" Julianne asked.

The two Pelegians looked over to Buerna, who stepped forward. The silence before she spoke seemed to go on forever, as if each passing moment stressed the importance of her next statement.

"You must leave the system."

"Do you care to elaborate?" Slydin asked.

"The answer to solving this issue lies elsewhere in the universe. Based upon the collected wisdom of the Elders, the star charts of the Saro outpost and the statistical probability calculations of the citizens of Arphaxad, there is a place where the universe reflects upon itself. If we can find that place, we can find a solution."

Yirhan nodded. "We know enough that certain a place like this exists, but do not have its proper coordinates."

"This is nonsensical," Slydin jumped in. "A point in the universe? Why not just ask us to count every grain of sand on the beaches of Ripath? What reason do we even have to believe this mythical point exists?"

Buerna stepped forward once more.

"A civilization there contacted us, but the details have been lost. It was a message received generations ago on the Saro outpost of the Mizraim system."

"The stargazers? Why didn't they tell us the details?" Slydin asked in frustration.

"They're all dead."

Silence.

"How?" Mane asked.

"For all their brilliance at observing the stars, they failed to calculate the trajectory of an incoming meteorite. Their calculations were off, again the same problem as all the planets are having, and by the time they figured it out, it was too late. They couldn't gather enough life ships to save their entire race, so they decided to perish together."

"Their final act was to send us their greatest achievement: a storage system with all their collected knowledge and star maps of the universe. What we've deciphered is that they narrowed the search down to a small cluster of galaxies. We would be able to program this into your ship to aid you in finding the planet."

Behind him, the image changed to maps of galaxies with

calculations scrolling down the side. Dotted lines traversed the screen to indicate possible paths.

"Hold on," Slydin jumped in again. "I have a damaged ship. We have no capabilities for travel outside of our system and you want me to venture out into the unknown in hopes of finding a planet in a cluster of galaxies? Are you listening to yourself?"

Yirhan stepped forward.

"The Jericho would require some modifications and according to our contact on Bavel, they have something there that would assist you. To get the necessary technological upgrades, however, will be a task."

"You don't say," Julianne replied. "I suppose your engineers haven't invented it yet?"

"They're invented, but they happen to be on Mizraim itself."

Slydin threw up his arms in repulsion.

"A race of people who want nothing to do with anybody," Slydin said while shaking his head. "I don't see how all of this is enticing us to go on this ludicrous mission."

"What other choice do you have?" Buerna asked. "You have three options: Get captured by those in the Federation who want to use you as a scapegoat for their gain, keep running while watching the system destroy itself, or you can attempt to find that planet and save us all."

Slydin wasn't convinced in the mission to the unknown, but he was willing to travel to Bavel to see what they offered. It was as decision he was now regretting.

Prior to their departure, the Pelegians outfitted the Jericho with provisions for the crew.

"Before you go, we are going to give you a prototype of the portal device alongside its technical schematics. If there's a way for you to fix it along your journey, you can use it to get back home. We've pre-programmed it with the coordinates of this system in mind."

"You're assuming I will be going," Slydin replied.

"After you leave this planet, we cannot have you land here again," said Yirhan.

This stunned Slydin, who stood there trying to process what was just said.

"Members of the Federation Council will come looking for you here. We're giving you the prototype in the hopes it can be fixed properly, while publicly banning you from taking safe haven here in order to protect our people."

"You're sentencing me to death," replied Slydin.

"That sentence was already on your head."

There was no goodbye afterwards. They took off leaving Slydin to mull over their potential avenues for keeping the crew safe. He felt there had to be others in the system who would take him in and believed his fate should not be tied to his family. As much as he tried convincing himself of that fact, having Julianne on board the ship always reminded him how untrue it was.

Their arrival on Bavel was met with silence.

Julianne, Mane and Slydin stood at the exit ramp of the Jericho as they looked out into the endless sea of flat, grey landscape. Even the sky was a scorched red, adding to the depressing nature of where they had landed.

"It's so barren," Mane said, breaking Slydin's thoughts.

Stepping off the ship, the landscape felt as sterile as it looked. Each step felt like walking across a lifeless mural painted by an artist who gave up on life. In the Federation, secession had always been a problem, but for the lonely planet of Bavel it had taken a tragic blow. This nation had been one of the first that suffered a violent attack from Edom, the early leader of the movement. Being in the outer rim, security was non-existent. Once a host of large ancient towers sprawled over its surface, now, only the foundations of their majestic buildings remained.

The Federation proposed a relief fund but with the war dragging on, the aid never reached its destination. Slydin wondered to himself if he, as a Federation Ambassador, would be welcome on this planet.

Two figures waited in the distance. They blended in with the scenery, completely dressed in black cloaks and sported long black hair that extended just past their shoulders. Based on their figures alone, it was difficult to differentiate one from the other. Their pale skin looked as if the nearby sun had stripped them of their health.

"Greetings," Slydin called out.

"Greetings Captain Slydin," one of the figures responded. His mouth moved slowly, each word being carefully enunciated.

"Welcome to Bavel," the other figure said. This voice was similar, but at a slightly higher pitch. "I am Menrina and this is Drast."

"Thank you for allowing us to land," Slydin replied.

"It is in our best interest," Drast said. "I understand the Pelegians have briefed you, but are you aware of the strength of Bavel?"

Slydin turned to Julianne and Mane for information, but both of them shrugged at him.

"Your hesitation to answer," Menrina said, "is an indicator of your personal blindness. Why make the trip here if you do not understand what we offer?"

Julianne jumped in. "We have nowhere else to go."

The two figures stood still and carefully turned their heads toward one another. They whispered for a moment, then turned back.

"Are you not the cause of the recent war that broke out?" Drast asked.

Slydin slumped his head and breathed out heavily.

"Do not be hard on yourself, Captain Slydin," Menrina said. "The commodity we offer to the rest of the system is Ashem. A mutable substance that can be transformed into any other metal as needed. Its qualities are of the highest caliber to withstand even the greatest amounts of pressure. Have you ever wondered what the Federation's ships have shielding them?"

Mane's mouth opened slightly at the revelation while Julianne and Slydin shook their heads.

"How did you avoid an attack from Golates if the substance was so invaluable?" Julianne asked.

"Our planet stopped producing it," Drast answered.

Menrina nodded. "We invited you here because we want to offer something of greater value to your mission. Ashem is our only resource, however, since ancient times we've had another technology at our disposal."

Drast dug into his cloak. From the inside of a deep pocket, he produced a small book and presented it to Menrina. She took the book in her hands and gently massaged the cover while running her fingers along the spine.

She held the book out so they could see it.

"This is AshScript," she said.

"Your entire fortitude of knowledge and literacy," Drast began, "is built upon the discovery of this AshScript. It was the original language that allowed us to transmit ideas from one generation to another, without needing to resort to translations in different tongues."

"This is a cipher for a language?" Mane asked.

"Listen carefully," Menrina said. "This is a language that adapts to the desires of the person who is reading it. With it, you can see beyond the text and into the heart of what the writer is saying. If your desire is strong enough, you can read the secrets of the universe..."

"We have kept it a secret because of the power it wields," Drast said. "With this text, any message can be sent in its most simple form and be fully expanded to the one who wants to read it."

"The problem with the language," Menrina continued, "is when it's used for the sole purpose of benefiting the self, it can consume a person."

Captain Slydin's mouth dropped. *So, first we get a broken portal, now, an archaic book full of hidden fortunes. How the hell did my life come to this? I'm being hunted like a criminal.*

"What do you want us to do with it?" he asked.

"Should you make it to the planet you seek, we ask that you write down what you learn so future generations may benefit from it. Unfortunately, none of us from Bavel will be able to know about it."

"Are you concerned none of us will make it back?" Julianne asked.

"The people of our planet are all going blind," Menrina replied. "We are the last few who still have most of our vision intact."

"In addition to this script," Drast said, "we will also share the secrets of how to use Ashem to augment your engines to achieve deep space travel. We kept a reserve of it to trade for provisions. For your endeavours, you will need to take all we have. However, to fully use it, it will require the use of another power source. This will be the most difficult task."

"Let me guess," Slydin said. "We'll need to convince the Mizrian to give it to us."

Drast nodded. "We may be of help. If you're willing to make a stop on the planet of Diklah, we think you'll have a chance."

"But what about your nation?" Julianne interjected. "If everyone is blind won't you need massive aid? Your world will be destroyed."

Drast's face remained solemn, giving a grave response.

"Nothing can stop that now."

Walking Into Certain Death

"We don't stand a chance, do we?" Crimron asked Slydin as they boarded the Jericho after their briefing with Drast and Menrina. Slydin stopped him and motioned for him to follow to a more private spot on the ship.

"Crimron, listen, back at Javan, it was never my intention to put you in danger. You understand that don't you?"

Crimron stared at the floor for a moment, then eyed Slydin directly.

"It made me think," he said.

"I've always wanted to have a family. That moment, if things had gone the wrong way, it would have taken my life. With all that's happened, even now to raise a family with a normal life seems pretty slim."

Crimron saw how his Captain was tortured by his fallen face despite Slydin's attempt to remain unaffected.

"Captain, if you decide to continue and if somehow this is successful, we can be part of the reason others can have families. This is an incentive to not die, Captain."

"Thank you, Crimron," Slydin replied.

Crimron nodded, but didn't reply. He walked out and back to the bridge of the ship to get ready for departure, leaving Slydin alone in the room with his thoughts.

With so much weighing on his decisions, his mind felt like it couldn't handle any more. He wanted room to breathe, but being on the run, it wouldn't happen. His options to stay behind were also becoming limited. Everything rested on the information they were fed about the Diklan people.

Julianne found him and put her hand on his shoulder.

"How can you stay so strong?" he asked her.

"Deep down, as much as I loved her as well, I knew she had her reasons," Julianne answered. "I don't believe she was betraying the Federation at all. She knew something."

"How do you know?" Slydin asked.

"I don't, but it's the only hope I can hold on to. We have to do this, Slydin."

After a few moments in silence, they returned to the bridge and set a course for the planet.

"Mane, I want you to keep scanning the frequencies for any rogue communication. The planet of Diklah has no technology to communicate, which will allow us to focus on anything else that might come our way."

"Should we attempt to contact the Mizraim people now?" Julianne called out. "At least give them a warning we are coming, before we show up on their door?"

"We're not contacting them unless we have something substantial to say," Slydin replied. "They've been insular for so many generations, there's no telling what kind of reaction they will give."

"Captain, I'm already getting a reading," Mane announced.

"What is it?"

"Federation chatter. It's faint, but they have ships in the outer rim now."

"Intercept as much of it as possible and find out what they're up to. That's your entire focus, understand?"

"Yes, Captain."

Slydin felt crushed. He couldn't help but think he was about to get his entire crew killed.

THE CHILD OF DIKLAH

The planet of Diklah was a marvel to see. Given the sparse population of the planet, and their reluctance to communicate, this became an onerous task. However, Mane was confident at the landing location and Slydin had to trust him.

The colours of the land were a dizzying array of vibrant blues and greens, with a touch of purple. There were some landmasses that could not be identified as valleys or craters, but they were filled with such colourful foliage that it didn't matter.

All languages surrendered at any description of Diklah's beauty as it rushed over the awareness of any onlooker. Seeing the melded array of the planet's vegetation, one couldn't help but stare in silence, not wanting to break the visual.

Slydin and Julianne left the ship, inhaling the freshest air of any planet they had ever been on.

"Where to now?" Julianne asked.

"We scout the area," Slydin replied. "This is where most of our raw materials for the Federation's medical development are cultivated. We're bound to find someone here."

The scouting mission turned into a pleasant hike, allowing for time to admire the scenery. The wind began to pick up and while it felt soft on the face, they were forced to turn from it.

As their heads tilted, they noticed a clearing in the foliage and some figures moving around in it. They were low to the ground and unrecognizable from any other animals, carefully treading in a circle.

Every few steps, they would stop and bow their heads lower to the ground, sniffing it. Their hands, which were oversized claws, would then carefully pat the soil beneath where they stopped.

"What's going on?" Julianne asked.

"I don't know," Slydin replied.

They continued to watch and moments later, whispers came from the creatures themselves. They were soft, but audible enough for the two to hear.

"Are they speaking our language?" Julianne asked.

Slydin shrugged and leaned in closer, hoping the slight motion would allow him to hear something clearer. As he did, the wind suddenly picked up again and the creatures all poked their heads up to gaze in their direction.

Their appearance was off-putting to Slydin, who felt was as if the beings had not quite evolved into walking, but stayed low to the ground all their lives. After being stunned by the appearance, his instinct to wave a greeting was cut off by surprise as one of them stood upright and initiated conversation.

"Pleased to meet you, visitors."

Slydin and Julianne didn't know what to make of the greeting. The figure motioned to them once more.

"Please do not be afraid. We are aware that our posture seems a bit strange."

Its voice was deep and coarse, but every word expelled

from its mouth was thoughtfully precise making for a strange eloquence that was comfortably reassuring. The other figures in the clearing continued to do their circuit, occasionally picking at the ground.

Slydin stepped forward to greet them.

"I am Captain Slydin and this is my First Officer, Julianne."

"A pleasure to meet you both," the figure said.

It didn't stand completely upright, but rather leaned back on its legs, huddled low.

"I am Dormere, but do not have a title associated with it," he said. "Those you see behind me are part of a larger clan that oversees the children of this planet."

"You're looking after children?" Julianne asked.

"We are trying," Dormere replied. "With all that is happening in the system, all of our children are dying. We do not wish to further harm ourselves in trying to cultivate more."

"Cultivate?" Julianne questioned.

"Our ways may seem foreign to you, but we of Diklah have fully connected with the roots of our planet. The entire landmass is a living entity that we are only a part of and yet, a necessary component to keep it functioning. We do not communicate with technology, but rather with the systems already in place upon the creation of the land. The wind told us of your arrival and let us know you mean no harm in coming."

Slydin and Julianne stood there, trying to think of how to reply.

"I can see your minds working hard," Dormere said. "It does take some getting used to that your home can be a living, breathing place that requires the utmost respect. The more you give it, the more it returns to you. However, I am sure you did not come here for a lesson in morality."

"We were sent here from Bavel," Slydin said. "We were told you may have the key to helping us establish a connection with the people of Mizraim."

Dormere nodded at us. "Ahhh... yes..." he began. "We are

told they are a difficult people to communicate with, especially with their end coming soon."

"With all due respect," Julianne said. "What are you talking about?"

Dormere took a deep breath in and held it for a moment. He wasn't trying to contemplate what to say, but rather trying to ensure he had all the air he needed to finish everything that needed to be told.

"While the system and a few of our neighbours in the outer rim have used their technology to make calculations among the stars, we have sought another avenue of communication. We peer into the heart of all that is living and attempt to move beyond it. It was determined even from ancient days that all life mirrors a cosmic connection. This system permeates existence and its beginning is mirrored in its end. Just as our planet is dying, so is theirs. What is it you seek from them?"

"The technology to power the material for our engines," Slydin said.

"The people of Bavel must really trust you if they offered up their only resource," Dormere replied. "What favour did they request of you?"

"To find a planet somewhere in the universe," Slydin said while rolling his eyes.

Dormere eyed him, but didn't speak.

The silence evolved into high levels of discomfort before he broke it again.

"The planet that reflects upon itself?" Dormere asked.

"How did you know?" Julianne asked.

"The stargazers of Saro used to tell us their stories as they came here for shipments of food. We were the first to know about them being contacted and the last to know of their death."

There was another silence as Dormere bent his neck to the ground and contemplated.

"We will help you on your journey," he said, keeping his eyes to the earth. "We offer the last vibrant food source of our planet, which can renew itself in the conditions of your vessel. Provided, of course, you do not consume too much at once. We will also give you what the people of Saro requested, but their brothers and sisters of Mizraim were too proud to ask. In return, we ask just one favour."

Dormere stared straight at Slydin.

"Take one of our children with you. Should you find the planet, our child of Diklah will be able to commune with the cosmos in a way that none other in our system has been able to."

"One of your children?" he asked. "We are not equipped to take on children in our ship and it would be inhumane to separate the child from their parent."

Dormere had a blank stare and turned around to motion to one of the others. The other Diklan, who was busy with its head close to the ground, nodded and began scooping the soil with its hands.

"You will understand in a moment," Dormere said.

After scooping, the Diklan uprooted a small plant and packed the base of its roots with the soil from the ground. It was brought over to Dormere, who carefully took it within his arms and whispered to it.

"This is a child of the planet," he said. "Take care of it and should you find the planet, allow it to be adopted by its new parent."

"The plants are children of the planet..." Julianne said, beginning to understanding it all.

"Yes," Dormere responded. "It's too late to save us, but you can still save our future generations."

"Captain, we have an issue."

"Go ahead, Mane."

Already on board the Jericho with all the provisions need-ed, the crew formulated a plan to get in contact with the Mizraim. Most of it depended on Mane being able to break through their communications silence and present an offer to entice them. Slydin's only concern with the plan was Mane's major role in being the one to convey the message.

"The Federation ships are taking a wide orbit outside of Mizraim."

"They're setting up a barrier," Julianne said. "They know we're coming."

"It's more than a physical barrier," Mane replied. "They're blocking all transmissions to the planet."

"What about Peleg?" Slydin asked.

"They have a presence there as well," Mane replied.

Slydin turned to Julianne. "What do you think?"

Julianne examined the screen on her station, following the markers Mane setup for the sources of his communication pings. She began to follow the paths of the ships with her fingers, mesmerized by their patterns.

"Mane," she called out. "Can you hear any chatter from the planet itself?"

"It would have to be a powerful source and with the Federation ships circling…"

"Can you do it?" she interrupted.

He began to swipe at the controls at his station, working to pick up any signal the planet would be offering. Julianne moved over to his station and the two began to work in tandem. Slydin wasn't sure if his presence among the two would be an intrusion so stayed behind until he could be told what she was thinking.

"There is a signal and I can read it intermittently," Mane said.

"How much data can we send during those periods?"

"Given the timeframe of the interruptions and the blockade, it would be minimal."

"Send them this information at the next opportunity."

She typed something up on his station and a small string of data appeared. Slydin went to read it and could only understood part of the message.

"Are you sure they're going to be able to interpret that code?" he asked.

"It's not a code," Julianne shot back. "It's the chemical formulation for what they need. The last digits are a signal that we have it on the Jericho."

Mane held his hand over his station, waiting for the pattern Julianne observed to take its course. They were still too far out for the Federation ships to get a visual on them, but catching one of their signals would give away their position. Timing was everything.

He waited one full orbit of the ships around the planet… then two… then three…

"Mane," Slydin coaxed. "Are you going to send it?"

Mane ignored him, counting the number of passes and

watching his screen carefully. After seven passes, he sent the code out to the planet.

"What will happen if it misses?" Slydin asked.

Julianne turned to him. "Captain, that's your decision."

They watched as the Federation ships continued to circle the planet. Suddenly, Mane gasped.

"What happened?" Slydin asked.

Mane began to swipe away at his station. "The Federation signals are gone," he said. "I don't understand; they're not even broadcasting on their emergency channels."

"Did they go dark?"

Their conversation was interrupted by an incoming hail.

"Captain, it's coming from the planet."

"Put it up."

The communications system went live and Slydin straightened himself.

"This is Captain Slydin, of the Jericho."

"Captain Slydin, all Federation ships have been eliminated. You may proceed to the planet at these coordinates."

The bridge went silent. Slydin's jaw hung slightly open.

"Eliminated? What did you do?"

"Finish what your mother started," the voice stated defiantly.

The tension on the bridge hit an entirely new level of worry.

As they made their way to the planet, Slydin knew it was all over. They were being welcomed as sympathizers to his mother's cause, while starting a war with the Federation at the same time. He had committed them all to a death sentence.

Once the planet came in sight, they could see the dismembered hulls of the different Federation ships still orbiting the planet.

"What could have possibly done this?" Julianne asked.

"Nobody knows the technology the Mizraim people have kept to themselves. The Federation never asks and they have never caused any trouble."

Slydin remembered learning about this nation in his youth at the academy of Hellas. The oldest nation, according to legend, had once ruled an empire that stretched across the galaxy, even further than the reaches of the Federation. Despite their superior developments, they were overcome by a great plague that left them entirely ruined. Unable to recover, they retreated to their home planet and for thousands of years had been secluded from interplanetary affairs.

As an Ambassador, Slydin learned the particulars of every nation in the Federation but the Mizraim were a complete mystery. The Elders alone possessed the actual knowledge of how great they once were and what led to their fall.

All of them felt the eeriness as they passed through the floating debris. As they closed in on the atmosphere, Crimron through up his hands in frustration.

"What's wrong?" Slydin asked.

"They've overridden my controls," he replied.

"Mane, open up our communications again!"

"I can't Captain," he responded. "They've locked it down."

"How!?"

"Like you said, Captain," Julianne said, jumping in. "We don't know the technology they have available. Let's wait and see where this takes us."

Slydin realized it was a signal for him to collect himself. In this situation, the last thing the crew needed was for their Captain to lose control.

The ship broke through the surface and they could see the life of the planet below. There were pockets of vegetation scattered over a desert world. Farms surrounded a long river that seemed to stretch throughout the planet.

"Captain, I think I have something," Crimron called out.

Slydin walked over to his station and looked at the screen, which began to hover above showing orange points of light.

"What am I looking at?"

"Those orange dots represent a surge of energy that rides on the same frequency as our ship. My best guess is that's where they're broadcasting the lock down signal from."

"Can we get a visual of that landscape?"

"I'm working on it, Captain."

Slydin took a few steps back as Mane and Julianne came over to assist. The three of them scrambled to get something together and after a few moments, Crimron yelled.

"I got it!"

The imaging of the planet was pulled up and the points of light showed the structure of a pyramid with an iridescent green glow coming from the top.

"It's some kind of structural energy emitter," Julianne said. "They must be pulling from some energy source within the planet itself."

Before they could formulate a theory, the ship began to move once more. It began to accelerate towards the earth, angling itself towards the middle of one of the larger land masses.

"Where are they taking us?" Julianne whispered. "All their cities appear to be on the coastlines."

"Which makes the middle of the desert an ideal place to deal with issues," Slydin replied.

The landmass opened itself up to reveal a desert area. As they moved closer towards it, they could spot a huddle of towered structures in the middle of it.

"Is that a research facility or a military outpost?" Crimron asked.

"They'll have military at both," Slydin responded. "Whatever we promised them, have it ready for when we land. We're in no position to negotiate."

"Captain, we have what they need," Julianne shot back. "We're in every position to negotiate!"

"We give it to them or they take it by force," Slydin snapped. "Those are our only choices."

The Jericho was lowered along a landing strip just within view of the towers they had seen from above. A cluster of structures surrounded an obelisk that stretched toward the sky. At the top was a small satellite dish glowing a pale green.

"That must be their communications tower," Mane said.

"Can you read anything from it?" Slydin asked.

"No, my system is still locked."

Slydin turned his attention away from Mane toward the rest of the bridge. He opened his mouth to say something, but then shut it instantly. He had no words for the moment and instead decided to swallow the moisture gathering in his mouth. It was the only sensation his body could feel.

"Should we get ready to disembark, *Captain*?" Julianne asked.

Slydin didn't want to deal with the bitter tone of her address, but realized she had a point. He nodded in her direction and motioned for her to follow him. They waited by the exit ramp of the ship until the audible whirring hydraulics kicked in to indicate it was being opened.

Sunlight poured into the vessel, temporarily blinding the two. A wave of heat overwhelmed them as the dry, desert heat washed over their skin. As they took the time to adjust to their new surroundings, they noted a figure that stood at the end of the ramp. She had black, neatly braided hair and a slim figure. Her dark eyes were highlighted by immaculately well styled eye makeup. She wore a long white dress, with her arms exposed with what looked like a serpent-shaped circlet curling around her left arm.

"The medicine. Where is it?" she barked.

Her voice was sharp and had an air of annoyance behind it.

"I am Captain Slydin of the Jericho," Slydin began.

"The medicine or you suffer the same fate as the other Federation ships," she interrupted.

Slydin reached into his pocket and produced a small root. The figure eyed it without moving.

"A root? Is this a joke? Your message promised a chemical formulation."

"This is from the children of Diklah," Julianne said. "They used their last batch of good soil to produce medicinal components. I just gave you the formulation of what's in it."

The look on the face went from annoyance to curiosity. She walked up the ramp and took it from Slydin's hands. She closed her hands around it, brought it her mouth and began to chew.

A few moments passed and her body began to visibly relax. Her neck tilted slightly forward as her shoulders slumped down.

"Take me to your communications system," she said.

"Of course," Slydin replied. "May I ask your name as a guest on our ship?"

She grunted. "Ahaneith. Now take me to your communications system."

Heading on to the bridge, the crew stood up at attention to greet her. She walked past, ignoring them as if they were peasants in her kingdom. The power she commanded was breathtaking. However, it displayed her high level of arrogance, which Julianne took notice of right away. Mane moved aside before she could cross the room to him and pointed towards the seat. She barely paid him any attention as she sat down.

"This is Ahaneith, return stat call," she said.

"Go ahead first responder," the voice responded.

"Intel is good and promise delivered," she replied.

There was a pause, then a few moments later another voice came on the system.

"Bring them in."

She stood up and pointed towards Slydin and Julianne.

"You two are to come with me."

"What just happened? Where are we going?" Slydin shot back.

"The people of Mizraim are allergic to any other lifeform that is not native to this planet. Any presence of outsiders causes massive migraines to our citizens as our biological frequencies are tied to the power cores of this planet. An interruption of that frequency, which is what visitors cause, brings severe pain upon us. Until our facility can formulate the compound for all of us, only you two will be accepted into it. Your presence on this planet threatens our health."

"We mean you no harm," Slydin replied.
"Yet you brought us a war," she replied.
Slydin could feel his heart rate rise.
"We didn't ask you to attack those ships," he seethed.
"No, but your mother did."

"My mother was here?" Slydin asked. His voice went up an octave in the hopes of running into her again.

For the first time since their encounter, Ahaneith smiled. "No, but we sympathize with her situation. Now move."

The three walked out into the desert heat and along the path to the buildings in the distance. Each step weighed heavily on them as they were not used to the dry atmosphere. At first glance, it seemed to be a short distance. However, the road there felt like an eternity for Slydin and Julianne.

"Is this your research facility?" Julianne asked, attempting to make conversation.

"One of many," Ahaneith called back.

They finally made it to the entrance of the first building, which was a barricade of glass. As they walked through the doors, the cool, fresh air hit them directly and they reveled in it.

Even though the outside of the building would suggest a massive structure, the entranceway only had one glass hallway. As they walked along it, projections of different maps, video feeds and stats of the planet displayed prominently and were being constantly updated.

"What is the language being displayed?" Slydin asked as he viewed a pictograph of characters that scrolled along the top and bottom of the display.

"A language the Federation has forgotten," came the reply.

Ahaneith moved briskly, making it obvious she didn't want the visitors looking at the living displays prompting Julianne take a closer glance at the walls themselves.

"Slydin," she said. "There are people working behind the images."

Slydin took a close look and confirmed her finding. Many people were working at stations behind the hallway, but were masked by the images being displayed.

Ahaneith stopped at the end of the hallway where a doorway to her left stood.

"There are two people inside who never meet with anyone Consider yourselves special guests," she said.

Before any questions could be asked, she opened the door and motioned for the two to enter. Inside was a smaller room with a glass table taking up almost all the space. On its surface were the schematics for a device.

Standing behind the table at the edge of the room were two figures who were fixated on the work in front of them. Ahaneith moved to them and offered them the root she still held. They each took a bite from it.

"It is an honour to be here with you," Slydin said.

The three of them ignored the greeting and continued working away. Slydin turned his head over to look at Julianne, who looked back with confusion.

They began mumbling to themselves and Ahaneith acknowledged them once more.

"We are almost finished, then you and your crew can be on your way," she said.

"There are a lot of questions we need answered first,"

Julianne prompted.

Ahaneith looked annoyed. "You followed through on your promise and we want to send you on your way. It is not fit to interrupt a citizen of Mizraim while they are in the middle of working out a problem."

"And it's fine to keep a crew captive without any explanation?" Julianne blurted out. "Last time we checked, I think we've been the first visitors to this planet in eons."

Slydin's heart began to race at her outburst. He couldn't tell how they would respond.

"Captain Slydin, you keep good company," Ahaneith said. The two beside her continued looking down at the schematic ignoring the conversation taking place.

"What are they working on right now?" Julianne asked.

"We did a scan of your ship and its mission logs while we brought you in," said Ahaneith.

"What!?" Slydin called out.

"Many parts of your ship are ill equipped to handle such a long journey into deep space," she continued as if Slydin hadn't interrupted. "However, you are equipped with quite the formidable energy source for your engines. We are currently devising ways to retrofit your ship with our technology."

"Unbelievable. You stated before you sympathized with my mother. What did you mean?" Slydin asked.

Ahaneith's entire demeanor shifted to one of complete irritation. She stared at him for a moment, then began.

"When she became head of the Council, she promised to fix our planet's problem and then have the Federation leave us alone forever if we were willing to assist you in any way possible."

"How could she make that promise?"

"Perhaps I should just continue the conversation with you," Ahaneith said, turning toward Julianne. "He is too emotionally attached to the situation."

"We both are," Julianne defended.

"You can control it," Ahaneith replied. "You may leave, Slydin. Julianne can update you when we are done."

"I am the Ambassador Captain of the Jericho, if you want to speak about *my* future or the future of *my* ship you will speak directly to *me*," he responded.

The other two bent over the work table looked up at him. If Ahaneith showed serious signs of frustration, the two Mizrian could take it to a level that could erupt in violence.

"You will respect the wishes of The Lady of the two lands," one of the two said, "or the two of us will escort you out physically. It is bad enough that you are interrupting our delicate work, but now you also feel the need to aggravate the situation. Leave now."

"Fine, return to your work so we can leave," Slydin looked over at Julianne and muttered to her under his breath. "I want to know everything they tell you."

It was an hour before Julianne emerged. Upon reaching the end of the hallway she motioned for Slydin to follow her.

"What happened? What did they say?" he asked.

"They wanted to give me control of the ship," she said. "I spent the first few minutes convincing them you were still capable of your duties."

"Why would they get that impression?"

"The amount of chaos that's been following you. They've been following the Federation carefully since their planet started to become affected by whatever is destroying it all."

Julianne began to explain the problems Mizraim was having.

"The planet had prided itself on a technological superiority to others, having developed energy sources that provided an unlimited supply for the planet. They continued to innovate and advance, mainly focusing on increasing energy output. The pyramids had been their greatest breakthrough in being able to harness the energy field of the planet and use it for almost any purpose. While they did an easy job of bringing the ship in and maneuvering it around the planet the readings are now starting to decline, and the once powerful energy sources are weakening. The people of the planet are working diligently to overcome the weakness by seeking even greater developments and breakthroughs. However, they have been stalled by not being able to identify the problem that is causing this immanent technological failure. They are worried that when the technology finally breaks, they won't be able to continue forward. That's when Shelah showed up and offered them a deal. They were willing to break their treaty with the Federation," she finished.

Slydin took in everything Julianne told him, mulling over the details.

"They forced our hand," he said. "We have no choice but to leave. My mother…"

"Did what she thought was necessary," Julianne interrupted. "We either stay, keep running and try to avert a war that's already happening, or we become ambassadors to the rest of the universe. Even the Mizrian believed she was thinking with a higher purpose. The Council can no longer function without the Elders. It needs something greater."

"And we're going to do this with a broken ship?" Slydin asked.

"They are equipping us with a special device. It's a pyramid that recycles power and boosts its energy output. It will extend the life of the ship beyond the lifespan of any of us on board."

"You seem confident about the success of this mission," stated Slydin.

"More confident than what would happen to us if we were to stay here. They'll be done in a day and will send drone ships to distract the rest of the system," said Julianne.

"We're walking into uncertainty."

"Aren't we always?"

. . . .

"Do you think they told him the ships were empty?" Jandin asked.

Yirhan shook his head. "Even the Mizrian know what's at stake. I'm still puzzled as to why you chose this route."

"I had to force his hand," Jandin replied. "He had to believe he had no other choice. Otherwise, he would've been captured and given the same fate as his mother."

"You may have just sentenced your friend to death."

"The Elders were convinced he would be successful."

"What do you think?"

Yirhan and Jandin stood together as they watched the video feed of the Jericho leaving the system.

"I have hope."

Part 2

"Mane, gather our coordinates and ensure that pyramid device is working. I don't want to be floating in uncharted space aimlessly."

"Yes, Captain," Mane replied. "we are still connected with the Kitim infrastructure. After the jump, we won't need the Mizrian equipment right away."

"Captain," Crimron interjected, "on your command we are ready for launch."

Slydin recalled all his previous ventures. An entire series of unfortunate events that tied his closest friends to his own personal fate. His will froze for an instant.

He mentally pieced together the string of incidences that had led them to this moment. It seemed as if they had been urged on by some unseen force directing them to a final end and now to reach that goal.

"Punch it!"

The entire ship shook violently as the Mizrian engine sped into action. The crew braced themselves as the fierce shuddering seemed to threaten the end of their mission and their lives. The vibrations slowed as Slydin turned his head to the map displayed on the view screen, taking one last look at federation space when the sudden momentum of the launch tore Slydin from his sentimental recollection.

The shock lasted only moments as all the systems on the ship temporarily stalled, transporting them at immense speed to an alien dominion. The lights dimmed almost completely creating a dark ambiance broken only by the flashing of screens scattered throughout the bridge.

"Mane," Slydin called out, "how far should we get with this initial boost?"

"Well Captain," Mane started, "this should take us just past our star system. The Mizrian Astrography is superb. I wonder if they could have fixed the portal problem on Peleg? Do you think we should have asked them to look at the portable device we acquired from the Pelagians…?"

Slydin's blank unfeeling stare caught Mane's attention diverting him back to the subject at hand.

"…Ugh, right. Yes, we will be at the edge of known space. After that it will be too difficult to just rush through… Especially since we don't know exactly where we are going."

"Thank you, Mane," Slydin finalized.

Everyone sat in silence as the ship trekked through the cosmos. Nobody could speak. Only Mane took periodic breaths hoping someone would look his way to initiate a conversation. Slydin's concern for his crew deepened as it was hard to gauge how they were taking the situation. Their families and homes were now so far behind them.

After some time, a red light began flashing and the motion of the ship began to gradually slow. The lights reactivated separately until the bridge was totally brightened once again.

"Alright, where are we?" Slydin demanded. Everyone started typing speedily, drawing up astro-coordination and stellar cartography. Normally, the punching of keys would create a great white noise back drop allowing his thoughts too clear but the Mizrian had equipped them with virtual consoles.

Julianne spoke up. "It looks like we are on the edge of

known space. Not much further and we will be outside of Federation guidance communications."

"Why couldn't they have pushed us further?" Slydin asked.

"Well, due to the sporadic disposition of black holes and placement of the stars, not to mention comets and asteroids, this was the closest they could get us without having to guess for possible collisions," she answered.

"Crimron," entreated Slydin, "Keep it steady. Everyone else listen up. We know roughly where the destination system is and we need to make sure we get there safely. Once we pass the border of known space I want everyone to get some rest. You've all earned it."

"Captain," Mane stated suddenly, "look."

Looking over his shoulder his eyes widened at the display. All Captain Slydin's emotions returned at once. Immediately, he called everyone's attention to the rear view virtual screen that opened toward the entrance of the bridge. All chairs spun to face the life-sized map of the entire Federation planetary collective. All seventy planets and the stars familiar to them as children were now physically behind their position. The beautiful array of a cosmic harmony displayed live captivated the entire crew. No one aboard could ever have dreamed they would be seeing their home from this angle.

"Captain," stated a familiar voice, breaking Slydin's deep trance.

"Yes Crimron," he replied.

"We have left known space. I'm setting the auto pilot."

"Very good. Listen everyone: we are not running. We are on a mission to preserve everything you see. Burn that image into your minds. All of *that* depends on how well we work together now."

All present stood at attention as he made his departure from the bridge. When the door closed, Slydin could hear Julianne giving the final orders.

"Everyone, let's get some rest now. We all need to be in top shape. We don't know how long this will take."

Entering the captain's chamber, Slydin removed his boots and dropped onto the bed. Sleep came quickly and a darkness swallowed all conscious thought until his mental being matched the hollow dark abyss that now surrounded his ship.

Past the boundary of cosmic order and all certain understanding, our drifting unhindered sprawled down a pattern with no trails or marking familiar. Onwards, away from acquaintance and headed for uncertain ends towards a small point in the heart, leading the blind through the darkness in a place of complete restriction around that middle point.

Emerging from the vacuum, seeing a glimpse of the light far off to the sides illuminating his first thoughts clearly:

'What have I done?'

Slydin retreated out of the captain's chamber into the hallway. The lights had been powered down to dim so the crew could take a much-needed rest. Especially since it would be a long while before they passed into anything that resembled a colonized system. Entering the bridge, Slydin opened three surrounding holo-windows to display the outer space they were journeying through. It was a magnificent black. The scattered stars around seemed so far away.

How will we ever reach anything? How did things come so far? Back home, at one time they called me a hero. But even that didn't last long...

Three years ago...

A lone shuttle broke past a dense layer of fog that lined the atmosphere of the world of Magog. This small planet's surface was almost entirely covered by water and perpetual storms, with only two provinces separated by a violent ocean.

Looking out the window, Slydin let his thoughts wander, imagining a sudden ship failure. Taking an involuntary dive into the ocean would be a terrifying disaster. The creatures that dwelled in those waters were among the most fearsome in all the Federation and the idea of a peaceful coexistence was a foreign concept. The entire fabric of existence on Magog was an evolutionary line of predatory behavior. His chain of thought was abruptly broken by the announcement of their arrival.

The shuttle opened and even before exiting, Slydin could see the monolithic structure used to house most of the Federation's criminals. Stepping off, the swift winds lashed out with mist from the surrounding environment. A single robed figure flanked by visibly armed guards approached. Squinting his eyes against the blowing rains, Slydin quickly moved towards his host.

He motioned towards a guard who held up a small device, striking the top forcefully with his thumb, blanketing everyone in a clear light shield that deflected the rain and violent wind.

"Cahptain SSSlydin. I am Yajuj, Warden of the Ultimus. Pleasse come right this way."

The Scythian natives of this planet had never really surpassed their biological makeup. Seeing his long, stringy black hair from behind was an improvement from the presentation surrounding them. Their gumless jaws gave their face the appearance of a decaying corpse while their lidless eyes and gray skin provided a frigid look matched only by their callous behavior.

The large, metal gates creaked as they opened. Yajuj took the lead with Slydin following close behind. The thick walls that lined the construct were so broad it took a long while to pass them and enter the prison.

The gates gently scraped to a close as Yajuj wasted no time leading Slydin to the cell he had come to visit. There were no bars or windows: the two stood in front of what looked like a door carved straight out of the wall. The Captain stared for a moment, confused, as it seemed to almost be welded shut.

A virtual console appeared and a code was typed in by Yajuj. A full bodied holo-screen opened, presenting a visual of the fiery-skinned son of Lehav. Very few races in the Federation were as aggressive as the Lehavim. This one had committed several heinous crimes and was formerly one of Slydin's closest friends. It quickly became obvious that he could see them as well. He stood up and walked forward.

"Could you give us some time?" Slydin requested of Yajuj.

He motioned to the guards and they exited the area. Hardly a moment later, Slydin's repressed rage seethed mercilessly.

"How could you? What the hell is wrong with you?! What could have made you think this way? Why Esav? Why did you do this!?"

"I feel nothing but pride in my actions. I did only what was necessary for my people," responded the Lehavim.

"Weren't *we* your people?" countered Slydin. "We grew up together. We studied at the academy on Hellas. We lived there for over a decade. We were trained to be ambassadors. How could you do this? How can you take pride in *this!?*"

His head dropped slightly. His fiery skin coursed as he stood before his old friend. He breathed deeply before answering.

"Honestly, I did not know they would attack Hellas. But what is that worth now? No one listens to us. We barely have a voice in the Federation. We asked for help and who responded? You were there! My peoples plight means nothing to the Federation."

"And what now?" Slydin demanded. "What do you think you've accomplished with that stunt of yours? It was a school. *Our* school! Where *our* Federation trains its leaders. Where they trained *us*. On top of that, the migrants of the Reu sector were helpless. How can you possibly justify that?"

Esav looked indignant. Silently, he stared through the projection.

"My people have been heard. Maybe now *yours* will pay attention."

"What attention can you hope to have? It's over! Edom is gone. Your planets and their moons have been bombarded. After the Federation blockaded your nation, the remaining leadership spiraled the planet into another of its endless civil wars. None of *your* people are coming. It's only me now."

A deep silence saturated the space between the two. Esav looked somewhat downcast but still indignant. For the first time, he saw his best friend in a vulnerable position.

"I can't get you out, but I can save your life. I have the word of Elder Ronne. You can spend your remaining years here, but I need your help. Tell me why your people attacked Bavel and who supplied you with weapons."

Esav turned his head for a moment, looking toward the wall of his cell. He took a deep breath before responding. "You know… we get so angry. It's in our blood. We just don't get along with anyone. When I saw my planet suffering… when I saw how my people cannot actually occupy lands near every other nation… how we are segregated from everything. We never belonged in the Federation, even from the beginning."

"You know I understand. We are like brothers. I don't want to see you executed, but you need to help me. The weapons and Bavel," Slydin insisted.

Esav swallowed hard, looking directly into the display. "We attacked the system of Reu as they were being carted away. We hoped to displace them so we could occupy the outlying worlds and seize its sun for ourselves. I helped orchestrate the attacks on the civilians. As an Ambassador, I had intimate knowledge of their positions. I gave access to our fighters using my personal clearance codes. I do not know any more than this, but even if I did, I would say nothing. I will never fear death. I will share the plight of my people."

Esav shouted for the guard and after a brief pause, Slydin turned away. Yajuj came forward as the holo-screen shut down.

"Youuu know, we could torrrcherr him for the information."

Slydin was aware of the brutality of the people here and Yajuj's efforts to produce a common accent so the Captain could understand his offer.

"Not necessary," he replied, "there is nothing left in him worth taking."

After being escorted back to the shuttle, they took off. There was no way anyone would stay at that dismal place for any longer than needed.

Three Years Ago

"Any luck with Esav?" Julianne's voice broke past an intercom as the shuttle left the dreary atmosphere of Magog.

"Nothing. I really thought I could reach him. He's surrendered to the call of his bloodlines," replied Slydin coldly.

"I'm so sorry."

His thoughts travelled back to the prison cell trying to gauge another method of approach. *Could there have been something more?*

"Captain Slydin," Julianne interrupted, "there is the matter of the migrants. They will have to be repatriated to their home worlds. You're being summoned to the privy council meeting to discuss what to do with the reorganizing of the Reu sector. I'll greet you when you arrive."

"Thank you, Julianne. Keep me updated on anything I miss."

"I will Captain, and again… I really am sorry."

She signed off. The shuttle broke speed and headed through a grid portal that transported them to the second rim. The Reu sector.

With the dense planetary system of the inner rim left behind, the second rim system of Reu existed as a testament to Federation innovation.

The planet itself bordered the wide orbit of Peleg, the largest of all Federation worlds. When this orbit crossed within the range of the second rim, the lesser planets of the area would suffer from the gravitational interference. It threatened, at one time, to permanently disrupt the entire region.

Nine planets formed the basis of the Reu system and they all depended on the maintenance of an artificial sun to keep everything stable. As the centuries progressed, the planets became inhabited and expanded as permanent colonies. Only recently had there been problems with the ferrous metals used in Reu's generators. The gravitational pull had been failing and the colonies began to experience drastic weather changes.

Looking out the shuttle window, Slydin noticed the light-green planet they were about to land on.

So, the meeting is on Jorah.

This world he knew very well and it felt so strange to see it deserted. As promised, Julianne was waiting outside a spherical building. Stepping out of the shuttle, he approached her and she immediately began her brief.

"Everyone is here except the Ionians," she began. "The entire privy council. The Federation is showing a united front."

"You're sure having me here is a good idea?" Slydin enquired.

"Captain! You saved those people. If it weren't for you, they would be dead," Julianne affirmed.

"No, I if I had placed you in the right position from the start, none of this would ever have happened," Slydin countered. "Everything we did was corrupted from the beginning. If I am still Captain after this, I want you to take Esav's place as my First Officer."

Julianne looked honored and horrified at the proposition.

"Don't look so mystified. If things go as they should, I will be arrested and you will be a captain," he mused.

Inside, a long table filled with ambassadors, delegates and planetary leaders most of which were from the second rim, was amidst a heated debate. They went silent as Slydin walked in and took his place standing before them.

"Looks like you made it," announced Ayin, the Chief Ambassador from Gomer. His planet assembled the shuttles and spacecraft that took everyone in the system from where they were to where they need to be. "You can take a seat, Captain."

Slydin took his place at an indiscriminate part of the table knowing that the moment they no longer found him useful, he would be arrested. Julianne stood behind her Captain with her hands positioned behind her back, following an orthodox protocol.

"Do you have anything that may help us?" Ayin added.

Drawing in a deep breath, Slydin paused a moment, then clearly detailed his answer.

"There was nothing he was willing to give up. To tell you the truth, this looks much deeper than it has shown itself to be. I highly doubt he even knew anything of value beside the point of strike."

Everyone went silent, again.

"Slydin, we're not going to arrest you." Ayn continued, "If you had been in on this, even more would have been lost. But gentlemen, let me remind you, we now have to consider the return of the refugees to their home colonies."

Another delegate from one of the second rim planets broke in. "We also want an increased security presence to assure that *this* never happens again!"

"We are prepared to send four legions: two from Gomer and two from Sidon," Ayn responded.

A delegate from the far end of the table interjected before

the conversation advanced. "Also, out of respect for our people, we would ask that Captain Slydin be removed from these proceedings."

Some of the delegates present began to protest. Before any disagreement could erupt, Slydin rose, "It's okay. I completely understand."

Ayin nodded, "Captain Slydin consider yourself formerly relieved of any duties or responsibilities pertaining to this matter. Take your ship and return to the inner core to await further orders."

"Yes, Sir." Slydin agreed, then standing, took two steps back, bowed slightly, half turned and proceeded toward the exit with Julianne following close behind. While passing the entranceway, two of the delegates quickly caught up to them.

"Excuse me, Captain. Please wait."

His walking slowed and after swallowing hard, he turned to face them.

"Sorry Captain, for everything that's happened. You don't know us, but I am Jimi, the Chief Representative for Obal and this is Tikal, the Envoy of Shelef. Our families were on those transports. The ones you led to safety. They were not on Hellas. You saved them. What happened back there... not all of us think like that."

Slydin extended his hand, "I'm sorry I couldn't do more."

They both took turns clasping his hands, offering thanks with faces washed with gratitude. After finally exiting the building, Slydin had Julianne summon a transport from the Jericho. He wasn't going to ride aboard outside conveyance anymore. It was time to go home.

A Jericho pod arrived in short time and he and Julianne rushed aboard without saying anything. On the way, he peered out the windows and recalled how only a month before he and his crew had commandeered almost the entire fleet of ASH-Kenaz trade ships to load the Reuian sector's people to safety.

A month ago, I was a hero.

Docking the Jericho, the two marched to the bridge. The crew stood up as they entered.

"Effective immediately, Julianne is the Jericho's new First Officer," instructed Slydin. "We are to depart to the inner core outside of Tarshish. If there are any other questions, bring them to Julianne. I'll be in my quarters."

Julianne seamlessly took command as Slydin headed back to his room to get some rest. Upon entering his quarters, he took out a portable display and looked over some mail. Jandin had left him an update linking to recent Federation news:

After the destabilization of the Reu system and the subsequent displacement of millions of Federation citizens, an unprecedented tragedy escalated in the wake of Lehavim terrorism that claimed the lives of segments of the second rim population as well as exterminating many of the members of the prestigious academy of Hellas.

Mostly children and young adults, the students of Hellas were to be groomed by the Ionian Elders and Federation elites to succeed as the next generation of planetary delegates and coalition leaders. At the time, over three-hundred and fifty thousand refugees were stationed on Hellas. The students led the humanitarian relief efforts and aided the exiles.

As the Reuians settled into their temporary homes, a deliberate attack was launched by Lehavim rebels, striking at the vulnerable settlements. The academy was destroyed and now, not only have entire colonies been devastated, but the Federation will have to prepare for an inevitable leadership crisis within the next generation.

The attacks were primarily orchestrated by First Officer Esav, one of the principal figures in the evacuation. He has been apprehended and is awaiting execution. Captain Slydin,

Slydin mused over the article his colleague had sent him. *Jandin, you have a sick sense of humor.*

THE VOICE THAT BINDS

Present Day

Slydin's thoughts drifted back to his current situation. On the ship, the crew slowly resurfaced back to their posts and began to configure their location and destination. While entering, it was apparent that the crew's drive had substantially increased. A half smile broke over Slydin's face as he turned to Julianne who was also holding back her excitement.

"The Mizrian upgrades. They did more than just power the ship," she stated.

Taking his seat in the Captain's chair, he resumed order amidst the enthusiasm.

"So, what are we looking at?" he asked.

"The technology we are working with is greater than the Jericho's stock equipment," Julianne affirmed, "Not only does it automatically triangulate our position in the universe but it also gives us detailed imagery of galaxies and solar systems within the Mizrian database. Right now, we can analyze and actively seek out new systems and we are currently charting a course toward our mysterious destination."

Slydin was astonished at the prospect of not having to manually traverse dark space without Federation guidance. *We are now a fully functional, mobile space station and observatory.*

"How long until we find our target?" he asked.

"Not long," Crimron responded, "I *think*. We are still getting used to the new interface but since we departed from our original coordinates, the maps of the universe in the database have expanded considerably. We're working on it."

"What about the other systems?" probed the Captain.

Julianne spoke in, "Everything is completely automated. They thought of everything, from power supply to environmental control. Even scanning pods are aboard for when we arrive. How did such a society stay so well hidden?"

"Wow, the mission has barely begun and I'm already outsourced by foreign technology," joked Slydin.

Julianne, gestured with a slight head nod, signaling her Captain to follow. Slydin silently relieved himself of command to allow the crew to continue to accustom themselves to the new hardware. The two entered the store room where, to the great surprise of Slydin, the child of Diklah had expanded considerably.

"Don't worry," she said, "it won't swallow the ship."

The plant had adapted to its surroundings by spreading a system of vines over a wall and most of the ceiling. Its roots were still planted in a trough-like rack that would obviously soon need to be replaced.

"Slydin, come and see," she motioned.

From behind a counter, she revealed the book that they had been given on Bavel. It was completely archaic. Hard binding, with a thick spine. The entire cover was worn and except for antique collectors of supra-ancient articles, this item would not be of interest to anyone. She pushed the book toward him over the countertop. Eyeing the book, Slydin gently took hold of it, analyzed the binding and gradually, opened it up.

On each page was an engraving of three well-spaced rows of four letters each. He turned the pages slowly, carefully studying the dark foreign markings. Some had straight, sharp lining and others had more scrolled configurations. Slydin became more attentive to one particular figure. His focus drifted into deeper thought until a double vision spread over his perception forcing him to view the alien script in an even more arcane fashion. Slydin's eyesight drew out the lettering far apart from one another and as it happened, the straight edges of the characters began to merge into one another from across the page.

Abruptly, his vision shot back into focus. The letters began to move on their own, shifting as they systematically danced over the page.

"Are these holographic?" he asked, trying to determine the source of their projection.

"No," she responded. "These are far more advanced."

She spun the book, flipping to a random page and stood behind the counter facing Slydin. The Bavelim tome lay off to the side, but the lettering drifted off the pages and settled in neat rows between the two of them. Slydin smiled in surprise at the unexpected movement.

"Now, say something," she instructed.

"Ugh… Like what?"

"Here, I'll start," Julianne said excitedly. She took a small breath and just stared at the letters that were now permuting and shifting over the countertop. Where they had emerged, it seemed as if they were engraved into the very substance of the surface. Then, their colors morphed from black to lighter blue. Julianne looked up holding back her excitement.

"Read it."

"Juli…"

"Just… look at them and attempt to read. The rest will just happen."

Very quickly, Slydin began to notice that within their fluent motions a greater comprehension awoke within him. Staring down into the figures that were smoothly shifting before him, his hearing increased, thoughts slowed and the surrounding world became enhanced by a sudden newfound awareness.

The letters began to fill Slydin's entire vision and while he turned to Julianne, they dispersed. The letters had formed a continuous extension of himself through her and he also became a conduit of grace broadening her senses as well. This was beyond a general telepathy; it was a union of emotions. The letters were finding deficiencies and through their shifting, somehow were adjoining and enhancing the strength of those who perused them as one.

"Whoa! Julianne, we need to bring this to the crew."

Her smile confirmed what he already was feeling. The letters now joined with their thoughts, seemed to agree with the course of action and slid quickly into the book as the pair exited the room.

Emerging onto the bridge, Slydin called all present to attention.

"All right, all of you stop what you're doing and clear your minds as best you can."

The entire crew looked at one another in confusion as Slydin stood before them. He knew how odd this looked, but it did not matter. It would not be long before they understood.

Opening the book and slowly flipping the pages, the AshScript began to trail swiftly throughout the bridge, settling on the screens.

"Just focus on the lettering in front of you," Julianne instructed.

As they did the entire ship quickly registered what the fluid fonts began to perceptually describe. They all stared, quiet and uncertain.

"Sir, I fail to see the objective…"

"Mane!" Julianne interrupted, "focus."

Of course, it's Mane who distracts us from this perfect moment, thought Slydin.

The rest of the crew seemed to be completely pinned to their screens. The letters permuted in their usual fashion. Then, more began to emerge from the book. They covered the bridge in neat rows and swarmed the area as a strong red and slowly brightened to a light blue.

All present immediately began to smile as the joy of a new revelation filled their minds. Everyone instantly knew that the shapes of the letters symbolized the connection between one another and to nature itself. The AshScript became clearer as it re-wrote a corrected relationship among the group.

Despite being only the second person to see the script, Slydin found himself growing in unison with everyone. The more people immersed in the examination, the faster the development and the deeper the bond. The letters completed a sentence where language failed to speak. All, as one, underwent a neurosurgery that grafted them together.

The AshScript reworded the language of their souls and all reasoning followed closely behind. It became so intense that eventually the crew fell into a trance as their thoughts were purified. The adherence was made stronger by an emanating virtue coursing through the letters which engraved on their hearts. At this point a song sounded and no amount of speculation could conceive of its beauty, nor repeat its rhythm.

Slowly, the crew returned to their senses, albeit now with a profound link to one another. A common internal voice now bound them collectively. The letters continued their coursing over the ship, though now with a much less intense presence.

With renewed strength, everyone resumed work at their stations. It was as if they had all shared a mutual dream of reality at its fullness and had been imprinted with its purpose. All were peacefully silent. The crew simply dove into their tasks and while operating the ship, their closeness was reinforced.

Looking around, Slydin noticed Julianne had exited the room. He calmly followed, now having the additional sense of his mind's eye aiding him by its promptings to return to the storeroom, where he found her sitting before the Child of Diklah.

She had pulled up a chair and was sitting in front of the wall that had been wrapped in the outgrowth of the alien vegetation. The letters formed four rows of three, on a virtual screen and were permuting before her eyes. Keeping his distance, Julianne's face broke into a sporadic smile and her head would shift as if she was in a deep conversation, but no words ever departed from her mouth.

"You can come in," she said without turning her head. "I'm just hearing what our food source thinks about the trip."

"He can sense everyone on the ship," Julianne explained, "and he produces food for everyone differently. If someone has a certain nutritional deficiency or an inborn sickness, he can create a specialized crop that will ease their hunger and aid with their condition. And now, because of the letters, we can properly administer the food."

Slydin reflected over these past moments and how imbued this new consciousness was, how it made all of this seem so natural. Despite his mind being transformed, the basis of the transition still eluded him.

"It's not a telepathy," Julianne stated assuredly. "This is hardly close to the Ionian Elders. It's more of a logical empathy. I could feel your questioning but I did not hear any words. We can't know each other's thoughts. The letters create a sort of emotional speech that can be heard between us."

"How did you figure all this out?" Slydin asked.

Julianne gave a childlike smile. Turned the virtual console and floated it towards her Captain with the letters still shifting over it.

"I asked…"

"Why hasn't this been circulated throughout the Federation?" Slydin probed.

"Think about it," she replied, "it can extend the intuitive capacity of the readers in an almost indefinite way. These letters tie our desires together. What if you were united, but for the wrong ideals?"

Thinking for a moment made the obvious apparent.

"That's it," he exclaimed, shocked at the sudden inspiration. "Do you remember… three years ago, the attack on Bavel? Edom. He wanted *this* for his people. To stop the civil wars. He ended up nearly destroying the entire nation. He was after *this*. They refused help to rebuild their nation fully. They were protecting *this* treasure."

Both their faces dropped downcast as they became lost in their memories of a time passed and the lack of initiative from the Federation that had only made things worse.

Three Years Ago

"Tarshish?" Julianne questioned, waving to the planet in the view screen. "Are we actually going to land?"

"No," Slydin replied casually, "I answered a diplomatic request from their homeland before all of *this* broke out."

"Captain, those *beings…*" she broke off not wanting to expose her true reservations.

"They are part of the Federation, Julianne. As a diplomatic vessel, our prime motive is to respond to any needs of its citizen nations. Besides, this would be a break from our failings at heroic enterprise."

She thought it through and a slight look of uneasiness broke over her face. He understood why. Most people do found the Tartessos very unpleasant and when the initial request was made, the priority level was at low. Now, upon review, it had risen significantly.

The planet itself looked like a slightly misshapen rock just floating in Federation space. Completely barren and almost uniformly charcoal grey, the nation lived upon what looked like the most lifeless planet in existence.

With the pod prepared, Slydin and Julianne boarded quickly taking their seats. They sat in silence as the pod powered up and prepared for launch.

"Have you ever actually seen one?" She asked.

"Of course. I mean, it's hard not to. Where there is one there are thousands not far away."

"Oh boy," she whispered under her breath. "Well, you mentioned the request had become priority. Do we have details?"

A benign alert sounded and the pod took off toward Tarshish.

"Well, since Tarshish is a center for mineral and metal deposits, a significant amount of Federation resources are derived from this nation. As of late, they have been boycotting everyone. Since the attacks from the raiders, they have totally suspended all trading. Normally, these are simple trade disputes, but it has been months. This will start to affect production on all nations."

She thought about the situation and then reread the viewing tablet detailing the circumstances. After an uneventful landing, they exited the pod and found themselves standing within a desert that contained no sand.

"You sure anything lives here?" Julianne asked.

Slydin nodded and declared his presence.

"I am Captain Slydin, ambassador from the ruling council and Commander of the Jericho. We received a request from your nation."

…Nothing responded. Barely a breeze passed over the surface. The core's sun radiated without any obstruction, adding intense heat to the apparent desolation. Julianne looked around, pulled her comm-link and began to radio the ship.

"Put it away," Slydin said gently, "I've got this."

He stomped his foot three times and called out again. She looked at her Captain like he was crazy. A smile broke over his face as they waited for the result.

"Slydin… I don't think…"

Silently he raised his hand, encouraging her to listen.

A scuttling could be heard. Then from the distance, signs of movement became apparent although nothing but rock could be seen. Julianne now looked somewhat frightened. The scampering became louder and when it seemed to be surrounding them it suddenly ceased.

Slydin grinned, observing her uncertainty. Julianne quickly moved closer to his side. "Honestly, what's wrong with just stepping out and saying hello?"

From behind a rocky protrusion not far from their location, the ground seemed to shift and slowly move towards them. As it approached Julianne's suspicions rose. A large seven foot, eight-legged locust approached the pair. It rose before them and extended one of its limbs politely and which Slydin shook gratefully.

"Captain Slydin. We did not expect someone so famous to render a response." It spoke with a coarse voice and a benevolent tone.

"I am sorry I could not arrive sooner. The Federation wants you to know that despite our late reply, we are here to discover a solution for the needs of your nation."

The giant insect looked down at the Captain. He seemed to be pleased with the statement.

"I am Esharadon. I will be your guide. If you have questions, bring them to me. Do not wander. Our people get few visitors and it would be most unfortunate if you were mistaken for food."

He tossed his head backwards, throwing back a small grey tress of hair and led the two toward where he had emerged. He stood tall and vibrated his wings. It created an echoing sound like that of flapping paper, spreading around them and filling the area.

To the surprise of Julianne, the ground surrounding them, the ground surrounding them began to tremor as the insect inhabitants arose from the terrain. Converging on their position, a flood of eight-legged beings circled and curiously studied their guests. It was apparent that, despite the large amount of trade with the nation, many had never seen people like them before. The small horde crowded the pair and Slydin grinned as Julianne recoiled in fear. Seeing his reaction, she composed herself as Slydin turned to Esharadon.

"Looks like we're a big attraction."

He turned his head downward at a ninety-degree angle. "Many of them will never see another being from the Federation in their lifetime. You are a rarity."

He made some rhythmic sounds with his wings and the Tartessos scattered and returned beneath the earth in unseen holes.

"We have prepared an entryway more suitable for you," added Esharadon. "Please, follow me."

He took the lead and Julianne nervously edged closer to Slydin.

"You look a little scared."

She gave a dark stare. "I should never have agreed to come."

"That wouldn't matter," he replied. "I'd have made you."

Behind a large stone protrusion lay an opening. They looked at each other as their guide urged them to follow. Both stepped into the dark and as they progressed, the opening became more restricted. Julianne grabbed his arm as they proceeded down. Soon, the pair could see nothing but darkness.

"Do you see anything?" she asked quietly.

In response to her question Esharadon stepped aside revealing a light source before him.

"This way please, Ambassadors."

Together, the two emerged from a tight tunnel into a subterranean metropolis that spanned beyond their sight line. The entire nation had reconstructed their homeland into a super-community built on many levels. Small glowing crystals were spread throughout the entire expanse and openings into deeper reaches of the planet's interior were clearly noticeable.

The territory was alive with activity. Millions of Tarteshim were rushing in and out of different openings and there appeared no break to the traffic throughout the visible region. Julianne looked amazed at the ingenuity of the species before them.

"Amazing. So, *this* is Tarshish," she spoke quietly to Slydin.

"Tarshish," Esharadon broke in, "is more of a name given by the Federation. Among my peoples, we call our world-home, the Hive."

Both Slydin and Julianne, stared transfixed at the intricate design of a completely sculpted planetary interior. As if on cue, a rhythmic drumming resounded through the realm. In response, from another area, a hard beating began to set the tone. An explosion of music filled the nation. Each district was packed with Tarteshim suctioned to the walls of the tunnels, foraging with their upper limbs and with their lower, taking part in the instrumental composition that was now engulfing the Hive.

Esharadon led them onwards.

"They are greeting you in their own way. You see, our race is the last known species on this planet and we have evolved to be able to live off of its material. So much that our ordure, combined with our specialized abilities, have allowed us to constantly regenerate the metals and ores that were formed with the planet. We waste nothing in our nation."

"Ordure?" Julianne asked.

"Crap," Slydin responded.

"This whole planet is essentially built and maintained by the very substance that sustains my people. These are not so much mines as they are farms and with the surplus, we trade for custom technological developments and agrarian products we cannot develop ourselves."

The rhythmic frenzy had reached a new depth and the fantastic nationwide rhythm surged into an industrial concert with the whole planet as the stage.

Esharadon gave an in-depth tour of the nation's abilities. The Ambassadors rounded a deep tunnel and emerged into a mine. The music followed wherever they arrived and their instrumental creation constantly renewed itself with every region participating in the lasting harmony.

A live demonstration was given on how different metallic substances were farmed and then processed into alloys for Federation use. These quarries stretched on for hundreds of miles and were filled with Tarteshim. This nation gave no sign of a population shortage.

The two were then invited into long mine with a metal railway. The cart was made to hold the locals so it was more than spacious for Julianne and Slydin. Esharadon closed the door and pulled a rusty metal lever and the cart took off at such a speed that both of them lost their balance. Their guide extended four of his limbs and lifted them back upright. Soon after, they arrived at their destination.

"Sorry about the fall," Esharadon said as he graciously stepped aside, allowing them to pass. "I had forgotten that these are made for my people."

The two Ambassadors smiled, laughing lightly as they exited the cart, noticing the dimness around them. Small, glowing, shell-like container molds littered the ground in long rows. The music that had followed them had died down into the background.

Tartessos workers quietly moved about inspecting the shells, paying little attention to the visitors.

"This is one of our most sacred regions. These are our eggs, the most vulnerable of our society. Their lives are sacred and it was here that our problems began."

He escorted his guests to a vacant area, obviously once a habitation for a long row of eggs. Now, only charred markings remained of what were to be future children of the Tarshish legacy.

"The attackers forced their way in. They held our children hostage and made ransom demands. They stole our materials and the lives of our unborn sons."

"Was it Lehavim?" asked Slydin, unsure of how the Federation could have missed them targeting such a core planet.

"No, not the fire peoples. They used flame, but it was a dark, smoking technology. Something I have never seen from the Federation nations we normally deal with. We called for help repeatedly and no one came! So, the nation united and after the Queen gave the command for an attack and we pushed the raiders out. But not before…this."

Slydin turned to Julianne who had the same thoughts on her mind as he asked his question.

"What materials did they steal?"

"They demanded Uphaz." Noticing their confusion, he quickly filled in the translation from his native speech. "A specific osmium textile alloy. It's not an uncommon demand from the Federation nations of Togarmah and Gomer. When the nations we had traded with for centuries abandoned us and we lost a segment of our next generation, what else could we do but forcefully obstruct all of our dealings?"

Stepping onto the charred site, Slydin swept his fingers over the ash. This was the work of Plishtim flame throwers.

"You said you forced the invaders out? Did you keep hold of any that you destroyed?"

"No. We waste nothing. The many that died at our hands were consumed by our population," Esharadon responded.

Slydin stood silently, holding back an upwelling of anger.

"And we will supply no more of our products to the Federation until security is provided for my people," he finished, drawing Slydin back from my interior discourse.

"Not a problem," Slydin responded. "We will get you security. You know those particular alloys are used in high level fleet creation. Why haven't your delegates brought this to any of the high councils?"

"Our race cannot survive long outside of our home world. We do not produce space ships or high-grade technology. All of our communication comes from our trade with the Federation. Therefore, we have no permanent representation," explained Esharadon.

Slydin sighed, in the last month and a half, the only two emotions that he had experienced in any consistency were anger and sorrow, a trend that did not look to be changing anytime soon.

"I will get you a half legion of Rhodian soldiers for the assignment. Also, I will personally investigate this matter myself," assured Slydin.

Throwing back his grey tress, the large sentient insect seemed to smile, though there was no way of knowing whether or not his race actually could, or *did* show any definite expressive emotion.

"That is more than pleasing. This will be reported to the Queen's Council themselves. Captain Slydin, thank you for your visit. It gives me much comfort to know that my nation will have a dedicated Ambassador we can call on."

His body suddenly bent forward and his breathing became labored. He beat his wings in a rhythmic succession. Other workers stopped what they were doing and did the same. Then, as one, they approached the three of them.

"Every being born in the Hive knows exactly how many days they will live," Esharadon began. "We do everything we can to serve the nation as much as possible. Our limits are known instinctively and thanks to you, my last days were of use to my people. Captain, thank you for allowing me the opportunity to bridge the gap between our nations. My days were not wasted."

He folded himself up, tucked into what could only be

assumed was a fetal position and his body slowly came to a deep rest. The rhythms had ceased in the distance and the surrounding crowd grew in number.

A small group approached and began pulling off his limbs, wings and body parts. They divided him right in front of their guests. Slydin surprised fell speechless.

"What the hell!" shouted Julianne. "What are you doing!?"

Another stepped between them and their fallen guide. "This is our custom. Esharadon was a noble son. He will be consumed by the population and the Queen's Council. It is a high honor. We will waste none of him."

After the quick dissection ceremony, the crowd dispersed and the two were led back to the surface, still shocked by what they had seen. While re-entering their pod, Slydin's anger resurfaced.

"Slydin, we have to be absolutely sure."

Looking up at Julianne, he had no words. The whole Federation had either been blind or willfully ignorant.

We targeted the wrong enemies.

Present Day

He was running through the neatly manicured forest path, passing through the stream with perfectly placed rocks for stepping.

"Can't you run faster?" he joked, while looking over his shoulder back at her.

"My legs can't move like yours can," she responded as she brushed her waving hair out of her face. He could see she was sweating. Slowing down, he grabbed her hand and they continued together.

"Come on cousin, we are almost there."

They traversed uphill next, following the well-made signs that gave them a sense of direction and accomplishment.

"Look," he said, completely excited, "Here is a map. We follow this trail and up at this peak. This should take us back to home base."

The two both smiled looking at the peaks rating.

"Slydin. It's three point five. Are we allowed to go to one that high?"

"We are if no one tells us not to. C'mon."

Grabbing her hand, they raced even faster to their destination. At the peak, the pair stopped and viewed from a majestic height the manors in the valley below. Scanning the distance, Slydin found their objective and then pointed.

"There! Just like the map said. All we do is take the falls down."

"How many cabins do you think there are?" she asked.

"Well, this is Ripath, so… a lot. When we get back we can eat. I think everyone will still be at the hot springs, so we'll have the cabin to ourselves. You ready?"

She was nervous but repressed her fears as she nodded with a forced smile. As one, they approached the falls.

"I'll go first…" Slydin proclaimed.

She instantly cut him off by grabbing his hand.

"Oh. Okay, we'll go together."

"One… Two… Three!"

Together, they jumped into the falls and immediately the power of the current propelled them downward. Both laughed gleefully as they slid; the water rushing around the two added to the exhilaration. At certain curves, they were thrust outwards skimming the top of the side. When it looked like they would fly over, another dip eased their descent.

Coming to the bottom the pair laughed till exhausted and their lungs hurt.

"Wow. That was awesome," Slydin exclaimed. "How do you think they mold a waterfall into a slide anyway? Look at how far we came down. Did it seem that high when we were on there?"

"I don't remember," she said, wiping water from her joyful face.

"C'mon. Let's check out the cabin."

Entering, they both left a trail of wet prints following in their wake. The cabin's automated systems reacted immediately sending a glowing blue heat field that passed over the floors evaporating the water and over their bodies, drying them off.

"Whoa. I love that feeling," his cousin said. "Why don't we live here?"

Slydin checked the virtual menu and noticed that the fridge wasn't completely restocked.

"Okay, I put in a request. Our sweets should arrive soon."

They simultaneously dropped onto the oversized and highly comfortable couch.

"When I finish studying at Helas. I am going to work full time on this world, in Carpathea," he announced with complete conviction.

"I thought this was Ripath? And what about me?"

"Carpathea," explained Slydin, in the most refined tone available at his disposal, "is the only city on this planet, if you can call it a city. And of course - you will be my official assistant."

"Yes! Our lives are awesome," she excitedly responded.

"I know, right? It's nice when you have things figured out," he replied.

Slydins vision went blurry and the voices all molded into one awkward rhythm. Everything went grey as his eyes opened. His senses took over and he began to forget most of the dream. Rising slowly, he awoke more fully and left his quarters.

How long have I been sleeping?

He moved over to the bridge and upon entering, he was lightly greeted by some crew members who were finishing their shifts. Sitting at the Captain's chair, he called for Julianne to report.

"There has been definite progress. The Mizrian technology is superb at cosmic trajectory. We don't have an exact location but we have identified over ten thousand planets in a star system we presume to be our destination."

"You presume?" Slydin queried. "Ten thousand? These don't sound like precise calculations."

"True," she replied. "But it was a list of almost fifty-thousand-five cycles ago and now it is in one system versus three and our calculations are ongoing. It will not be long before that list shortens drastically. In fact, due to these advanced upgrades, we can see that list being cut down in a matter of hours."

Well, Slydin thought, *this may actually not be that hard. We spent the shift overlooking and scanning the universe beyond. Not just for our destination, but everything else surrounding it.*

The Federation launched many expeditions in their early years, centuries ago. They brought back many races and resources that aided in our home system's development. But the records were always kept sealed as to exactly where they came from and in the end beyond the outer rim was just too far to travel for any discovery to be economically viable.

Slydin ended up skipping a relief and worked over eighteen hours straight with the crew. In triangulating and analyzing a planet to have an unseemly disproportionate amount of life that matches the criteria of the Mizrian, already put together in their search for it.

With the list now down to less than two thousand and a course charted, the crew prepared to make a jump beyond light speed. At this time, Slydin retired from his post and left Crimron to the details. Returning to his quarters, he fell into bed as the alerts came on instructing everyone to brace for take-off.

Lying in bed, Slydin's enthusiasm for what they would discover faded quickly as a wave of exhaustion poured over his being.

His past once again emerged in a dream…

His first assignment as an ambassador found Slydin temporarily stationed within the nation of Girgashim, beings who had exhausted their natural world and recreated it from the inside. They controlled all of the settings for optimal agricultural growth from their subterranean world. They were completely self-sufficient and rather than compete with the plentiful supply from the Hamat nation, they leveraged a monopoly on glucose.

Their entire society was a complete reflection of their inner perspective. Bleak and dry, even after being brought into the Federation, they were fatalistic protectionists who belonged in the furthest reaches of the outer rim. Even the look of this nation's species was off-putting. Large craniums made up the bulk of their bodies. Exaggerated facial features made up the majority of their cranium, supported by stilt-like legs and flanked by two thin arms, with their being supported by stilt like legs, making the Girgashi a disagreeable sight by the standards of most Federation races.

Sitting in their homes was an even more obnoxious situation. Because of their extended fingers, food was set on tables barely passing the ground level with tall chairs constructed to pose them far over it, allowing their long snake like extremities to slither downward to scoop up the meal, pieces at a time. This caused any visitors, no matter how seldom, to always be sitting well beneath their hosts and this is something the Girgashi liked very much.

"You see my boy," explained the Girgashi host, "this is why the Federation is destined to fail. The entire web of planets the Elders have spun to create a necessity for each nation falls apart with even the smallest of secession. All of our being, no matter what race, exists on the basis of need to receive for the self alone. This is the foundation of how we perceive reality and this is how we govern our affairs. It all settles around our own self-interest."

Slydin's neck stiffened as he was forced to stare directly up at his host from the ground. Since this was his first diplomatic placement, Slydin had to oblige the nation's hospitality and customs.

"See, we, Girgashim, understand this. We never leave the center of our world and do you know why that is?" he quizzed, looking down at the young Ambassador with his large eyes, leaning on his tentacle-like fingers for support.

Slydin was not sure what to say. Swallowing a mouthful, hoping his host would just continue to talk so he wouldn't have to say anything, Slydin allowed an awkward pause to settle in and then the Girgashi smiled, revealing his studded, uneven teeth.

"We have discovered for a long time now, that our most perfect state is that of a mother and child in prenatal development. Our planet is our mother. She gives us everything we need to survive and has done so for thousands of years. Our symbiotic relationship is the only perfection in the universe. The Elders of Javan, *your* teachers, are delaying the inevitable. Since the inception of the Federation, all they have ever done is suspend the entropy that overtakes us all."

Slydin took it all in, unimpressed. How did such a race not just succumb to depression and suicide? His host consumed some food and then continued his discourse. His neck was paying an awful price for the sake of diplomacy as Slydin attempted to keep his attention focused on him.

"Life is and has always been, an accident. For whatever reason, the universe has not fully corrected this, but does so in small portions with death and conflict. In the end, all return to where they were born. *We* never need to return, for we live as all should have been. Tell this to your Federation masters. They can learn from us."

The sound of a prompt roused the Captain from his dream. He was dizzy and as he rubbed his head he realized what the signal meant.

We just came out of light speed. I have got to stop sleeping.

Julianne entered his quarters, "Slydin, we have a problem. You need to come, now!" Rising, still in uniform, he quickly accompanied her to the bridge.

"Aren't our lives awesome?" he stated, hoping to remind her of better days on Carpathea.

She smiled, "It's nice that we have so much figured out."

Three Years Ago

Marvelous architecture and well-spaced symmetrical buildings lined the scenery. This was not the heavily populated worlds of Meshech or the industrial regions of Gomer. Here was the heart of the Federation itself. The planet of Javan was home to the Ionian race, the first of the seventy nations.

The Ionian peoples were collectively referred to as the Elders. No race in the Federation was more respected. The Ionians had taken part in every conflict the universe had faced and were the main instruments of resolution. It was the Ionians who created and instituted the idea of a Federation of Nations that was developed and expanded to this day. Their wisdom and insight played the guiding role in the organization's hierarchy.

Walking through the city's clean streets, brought back memories of Slydin's youth learning under Elder Ronne. His federation uniform made him stand out among the wide formal robes custom among the populace. This was the only actual city amidst the villas and countless gatehouses spread throughout this planet. Everyone walked at an even pace. There was never any shouting or loud noise.

Being raised for most of his young life on this planet Slydin had no trouble finding his way to Sanctuary Prime, the housing for the eldest and wisest of the Ionian nation. His heart sank while ascending the familiar steps.

How could I have let so many years escape without even once returning to see the teacher whose patronage allowed me the opportunities that granted my position?

After composing himself and taking the first steps through the giant door of the Sanctuary, the familiar smells of the meditative incense brought forth a mix of recollections from his childhood. Passing by many Ionians, wearing their deep colored robes, they bowed slightly toward Slydins' direction, greeting him in their custom. Rounding toward the main chamber, Slydin ignored the surrounding beauty and sped up as he drew nearer to his destination.

Entering the room, he felt disappointment set in. In the seat where his beloved mentor Elder Ronne would normally be stationed, sat another, younger Elder. His benevolent gaze met his expression. A voice resonated in his mind as he formulated a greeting.

Captain Slydin, thank you for coming. Please, come and sit. I am Elder Philo.

The race of Ionians were telepaths and had no need of any voice or speech to make themselves heard. For this nation, the mind was a primary resource and it is what they had offered the Federation since its inception. It was slightly uncomfortable, but Slydin quickly adjusted to the conversation. What he had done mechanically in youth returned as a fluent telepathy that flowed forth from his mind's eye.

I thought Elder Ronne would be overseeing this engagement?

I'm afraid he is indisposed at the moment. He is well aware of the situation, as we all are. He left specific instructions concerning these circumstances.

Elder Philo slid an envelope toward him. It had Elder Ronne's seal on it and as Slydin examined the item, he wondered why his mentor wasn't here to greet him. His thoughts wandered, concerned that the effects of the catastrophe of Hellas may have made him keep his distance.

I assure you, Captain, no one here blames you for the trage-dy that befell the academy.

Oh, damn it. I already forgot. You're telepaths, thought Slydin, feeling like an idiot.

Yes, we are and not to worry. Elder Ronne is by no means avoiding you. He is currently engaged in a contemplative circle. We are contacting the Source.

The Source! *How long has this been going on?*

It has been nearly six months now. A lot is happening that the nations are unaware of. A system dis-balance. Many of the Elders council have even tried to intervene by approaching the key minds of the planets to psychically counteract the forces at play. But the worlds are closing themselves off to communica-tion. As of yet, we have not found a true solution for the con-flict that has consumed us.

The Source was the very essence of the universe and what actively created and held together the fabric of reality. Slydin recalled learning about it in metaphysics and universal ontol-ogy at the academy, to this day he could still barely fathom the depths of such a process.

Breaking the seal on the letter before him, he read its con-tents. It was now very apparent what was happening.

How long have they known?

We have been conducting an investigation for almost five years. Normally, the Elders can predict with a greater certainty the deficiencies in our collective. However, as of late, the com-plications have become far more numerous and sporadic. Due to the Elder's influence, we have always softened what would be hard blows to the Federation's civilization. Now, if this col-lective degeneration continues at this speed, we are headed for a crisis of such a magnitude no nation has ever been faced with before.

Sitting back, Slydin thought of the severity of the issue and what he had just read.

Elder Ronne was trusting me. But how can all this happen? The federation has always been so strong...

Slydin...

Damn. Forgot again. Telepaths.

Elder Ronne has tasked you with a mission. Our resources are heavily stretched with the academy destroyed and the threat of uprisings destabilizing certain regions. It's all in the letter. Remember, we need proof. Something substantial that we can bring before the Federation. Also, you will not be working alone. We will be sending you to make contact with our operatives.

Slydin took the letter and his leave. Passing through Sanctuary Prime and exiting the massive building, his steps slowed as he became engulfed in his memories. The sun was setting and in the distance, a group of Ionian youths were sitting in a circle, silently being instructed by a teacher who stood amidst the center of them.

The Ionians exist as a whole in every aspect of life. The eldest of the people share their experience and knowledge with the youth in a subconscious way. All of the information from a lifetime is passed very quickly, disseminated and refined according to the needs of the generation. As such, the members of the Hellas academy that were stationed on Javan shared in this.

Esav, we were raised here together. How could you have done what you did?

The Key and The Doorway

Present Day

No one took notice of the Captain entering the bridge behind Julianne. Between the alarms and the flashing red lights, the entire crew were focused on their screens, demonstrating the severity of the situation. Slydin took his place in the Captain's chair as Julianne returned to her post.

"Alright! Someone tell me what the hell is going on."

Crimron spoke up first, "Captain, we've lost power."

"What do you mean? Did we take damage?"

"No, Captain," Crimron replied. "Something is wrong with the hardware."

Slydin remained silent for a moment. All the crew had now ceased their works, waiting for his response.

"Are we in any immediate danger?"

"None, Sir," a crew member responded from the rear.

"Power down the main systems. Get a read out of where we are, turn the alarms off, the lights on and then diagnose what caused this," ordered Slydin.

The crew went to work quickly. The lights returned, but

with a dim glow. A visual map spread out over one display showing the surrounding area.

"Any information you have I would love to hear right now," Slydin added. "Where are we?"

There was silence. After a moment, Mane spoke up.

"Captain, we are definitely within the galaxy that holds our destination. The system is running slower, but we will have exact coordinates shortly. I can't accurately tell what the problem is yet, but we have been losing power since we made the hyperjump. I request we reroute our current energy supply so we can get a better visual and that we power down all systems, except for diagnostics, guidance and thermal controls."

Slydin looked to Julianne who shrugged before turning his attention back to Mane.

"With all those systems down, most of our bridge will become inactive. Will we be able to restart the ship after such an extreme measure?"

"Definitely," Mane answered, completely confident. "Also, it will be easier to isolate the problem once the ship is powered down."

Mane's certainty took over any opposition.

"Do it."

The lights went black and all the virtual screens disappeared. The lighting that returned only filled the bridge in small, glowing patches. Mane worked unhindered, totally dedicated to the task at hand.

Leaning back, Slydin's thoughts drifted again over their purpose. He looked at the crew, noticing that they were all completely still. Only Mane, completely occupied with his duty, had a virtual window open, which contrasted the dimly lit ship that sat floating in space. He swiped two windows aside that neatly minimized and horizontally organized themselves next to his main screen. He continued to work quietly, with all the crews' eyes on him.

Another two windows were swiped to the side of his virtual workspace and he took a deep breath in. He outlined his screen with his index fingers, making a square. The screen turned red and he pressed his hand against it. Very quickly, a massive flood of lettering flooded his visual. When it ended, he neatly closed the window and sat up.

Mane looked up satisfied with is work, his posture aligned as he made his announcement.

"Okay. I think I found the problem. First," he said, swiping one of the windows back in front of him, "the reason for our loss of power is this particular technology is based on planetary core magneto-relation. So, the further we travel from Mizraim, the further we are removed from our power source."

Slydin felt a harsh pain in his stomach. *After all of this, we are going to end up stranded in deep space.*

Keeping a stern appearance, he immediately began looking for a solution.

"How long till the power runs out completely?"

"Well, it won't run out. It will just run slowly. This technology is far more advanced than our own. Here, take a look."

He pulled another window to his center, struck some part of it and a large spread of the star system filled the room. A large holo-field stretched itself out over the bridge. Some crew members exited their seats to allow for a clear visual.

"This is *us*," he said, highlighting their position. "Now, there are billions of planets here, but the computer has narrowed them down for us. The longer we spend within this system, the faster it will find it."

He drew a circle around a part of the visual. The area he highlighted was almost opposite their position.

"It is somewhere in here," Mane continued, "Now, I know that this system is incredibly vast but the computer will have a permanent location soon."

"How soon?" asked Slydin, now eager to know their destination.

"Very soon, Captain. I'll alert you the moment it's discovered," Mane pledged.

"You talk like we can just sail in. What about power? That area is lightyears away," Crimron interjected, annoyed by the claim. "It's obvious we can't use light speed. Even when we know where it is, how will we get there?"

Mane nodded frantically. "Yes, you are right. But it has been telling me that we have everything we need, despite the power break. It has become enigmatic whenever I mention anything hyper-drive based."

Tilting his head to the side, Slydin thought about Mane's statement. He would have spoken, but Mane kept up his discourse.

"It's actually really odd. The Mizraim are incredibly advanced. They would not have given us a ship with faulty equipment and it just continues to say we have everything in place no matter how I phrase the question."

Now it became clear to Slydin, Mane had lost his mind. He quickly raced through protocol and knew he had to confine him to quarters as soon as possible. It was actually surprising this had not happened sooner.

"Mane, *who* are you asking your questions to?" Slydin queried.

"Well," he responded unambiguously, "the ship of course."

Julianne let out a controlled yelp in response. Slydin looked coldly towards her and began his approach to relieve Mane of his post.

"You can talk to the ship?"

"Of course! Haven't you been able to?"

Yes, he's totally lost his mind.

"How long has the ship been talking to you?" Slydin was now approaching his station while trying to keep a calm tone.

"Well, since the AshScript I suppose. It allows for living interaction," Mane answered casually.

"…What?"

"AshScript… Captain, didn't you know?"

"Okay. What?!"

"You can talk with the ship?" he asked again, now beyond frustrated and trying to hold back a stream of rage that should probably be turned against himself.

"Of course… can't everyone? Here, take a look."

With a slide of his finger, he displayed the shifting lettering throughout the bridge. Sitting back down while trying not to have an aneurysm Slydins' agitation burst forth.

"Why didn't you disclose this?"

"I honestly thought everyone knew?" Mane stated to his defense.

"Mane. If everyone knew, don't you think *all* of us would have used the AshScript as a medium to diagnose the problem?"

"Well… umm. Yes, that would've made sense."

Slydin gripped the chair he was seated in until his hands went numb. Taking a deep breath, his composure returned and the entire crew took their places at their original posts. Slydin immediately took over.

"Now that we have a grasp on the situation, Mane, power off the live map and restart the ship's systems."

After a short time in darkness, a prompt sounded and the lights activated. The systems were operational again, but they still had the problem of finding their way.

"How long till we know the location of our destination?" Slydin demanded.

"About twenty minutes or so," Mane replied.

"What about the hyperdrive?" he probed.

"Negative, Captain," Crimron stated, "we do not have the power levels to maintain jump speed."

Calling up a screen, Slydin peered into the letters and began to interact with ship. All of them were now united, not only as a crew with their food source, but also with the place that housed them. As he returned from the depths, the questions spun within his head.

We have everything in place. But we're losing power. How will we make it home?

"Everyone! Eyes on me. We will figure this out now," Slydin ordered as he turned his seat, engaging the crew.

"We know where the planet is, roughly. We also know we are at the opposite side of its star system. We have no hyperdrive use and have significantly less power than we did before. How does the AshScript, which never lies, continue to report that we have the means to reach our goal?"

The crew remained silent. No one had any more of an idea as to how to reach the destination then their Captain did.

"The Mizraim would have figured all this out. Something must be in place," Slydin rationalized.

Turning again to the letters. This time his questions were direct and his desires focused.

The key is already set and the doorway opened. Set your target and go...

What the hell does that even mean, thought Slydin. *Why was it now, that everything became so archaic when before it had been clear? What damn doorway...!?*

"The doorway! Peleg's gate. The Mizrian attached a gateway so we could move freely among the outer rim. We use the gate to jump us to the planet," Crimron exclaimed.

A sigh of relief spread across the bridge.

"Crimron, can you use the gate for this purpose?" Slydin inquired.

"Of course, Captain. But I will need to calculate our trajectory and location. We don't want to pass through a star or smash some planet that gets in our way."

"Good, you get on that. Afterwards, Mane, you check his calculations, then when you're done, check them again," the Captain ordered.

An alarm prompted the attention of the bridge.

"Ah, Captain," Mane declared, "we have the coordinates of the planet."

Leaning back absolutely satisfied with the current situation. The bridge was alive again and the confidence brought about by the discovery of a new world poured throughout into the ship.

We Are Watching You

Three Years Ago

The letter Elder Ronne had left contained instructions to seek to seek out help from the nation of Kitim. Slydin gave orders for the crew to station the ship within Federation space, while he and Julianne, boarded a shuttle from the Jericho and headed for the Kitim surface.

"Slydin," Julianne started, "what did they say?"

"I didn't want to tell you on the ship. Things are a lot further along than we had thought and I'm not sure who we can trust."

Julianne understood his caution. With everything that's happened, there was nothing Slydin was absolutely sure of. She was the only one he trusted, the only one he should have trusted.

"I cannot involve the crew on this one. The Elders of Javan have instructed me to aid in an investigation. Everything we do from this point onward is completely confidential. No command notes, no messaging, nothing. This is off the books."

"Understood, but what is happening? Is there going to be

another attack?" she probed.

"No, none of this is the result of terrorism," he explained. "This is part of a much wider conspiracy that endangers the Federation itself."

She was taken aback by the statement. Neither of them would ever have dreamed of living in a situation where the greatest and most stable power in the known universe could ever be undermined. She swallowed hard at the news. If the Elders were behind this declaration, then the truth of it burned deeply.

"What do we know so far?" Julianne questioned.

"Nothing. That's what we're here for."

After processing their diplomatic clearance, they exited the shuttle. The Kitim nation had very few natural resources, but in and of itself it was a marvel of the Federation. They were the last to be accepted into the Federation due to their awkward cultural norms. Kitim is a planet completely shaped by the use of trans-naturalist technology where anyone wishing for citizenship must first have their consciousness uploaded into the collective.

Julianne marveled at the nation she stood before.

"Slydin, it looks like a gigantic computer."

"That's because it is," he informed her, "All the people who live here are cyborgs. They co-exist with their nation. If a worker gets a contract on Kitim they require temporary implants to be able to commune with the collective programing."

A virtual screen opened up in front of them and displayed a message that was read aloud in a monotone, female, mechanical voice.

"Greetings, Captain Slydin. If you would follow me, please."

Both shrugged and followed the screen down a straight platform suspended hundreds of miles above the surface of the planet. Slydin knew this nation very well. All ambassadors did. The cyborg inhabitants were created from many of the races throughout the Federation and several of them were ambassadors from previous generations. Having proved themselves worthy, they were selected for a sort of consciousness based immortality with some of them being older than many of the Elders. As a result of their citizenship, the nation of Kitim had become staunchly loyal to the Federation.

The two were led into a large, cylindrical building. Inside, thick black cables lined the walls, leading into a single skeletal chair supporting their host; a bald humanoid cyborg, elevated by hydraulics began to lower. The bionic being's head turned the full way around as the chair slowly caught up with his motion.

"Greetings. I am Ciro, a representative of the Kitim nation. We have much to discuss."

His voice sounded like an echo reverberating through a metal tunnel. He did not rise or lower far enough to extend any formal welcome. Whether this was due to his automation or not was never disclosed.

"How much did Elder Ronne explain to you of the situation?" Ciro asked.

"He explained very little," Slydin countered.

"Very well," responded Ciro. He leaned back in his chair and three cords inserted into the back of his neck. His fingernails rotated revealing circled openings in his fingertips which also drew cords towards them. At this point, they noticed he was barefoot and his toes replicated the process his fingers went through.

In front of them, was an intermixed being that looked more like a bonded chain of cables rather than a living person. His eyes flashed a clear, shinning glow as over two dozen screens, some virtual, some physical, activated with various displays of coordinates, maps and stellar video feeds.

"As I am sure you are aware, our nation keeps control over the vast satellite networks that operate everything from navigation to communication and interactive processing. We have been monitoring a series of cryptic conversations that transpired over the course of the weeks prior to and after the attack on the Academy. This uncovered a vast conspiracy that is meant to undermine Federation activities. Most of our current data was disclosed by an undercover operative that has fed us information regarding this matter."

"You have an operative?" Slydin asked, surprised by the revelation.

"Yes." Ciro replied, coldly. "You will make contact with him following our discussion here. You will take one of *our* shuttles. You will not return to your ship, nor inform them of where you are going."

He thought for a moment and understood why they were called here. Normally, the Kitim security network picks up on any negative elements throughout the nations. If they need eyes on the ground, it means the groups involved had been eluding them.

"Which nations are most likely involved in this?" Slydin probed.

"From what we have discovered and from what *you* have recently learned, the Plishtim race from the nation of Casluhim have a major hand in dealing with the supply of weaponry. Normally, mercenary groups from this nation go rogue, but from what we have been able to determine, many high-ranking officials have gone off the grid. They are doing their dealings directly or have been coerced in some way to become involved."

"If you know these are happening on Casluhim, why not send an extraction team?" Slydin reasoned.

"The Casluhim nation and its surrounding moons are heavily polluted. Most of our people would die within hours upon landing without proper gear. The world is packed with factories, some of which emit carbon exclusively for the sake of the populace, which thrives in that sordid environment.

We have no easy way to access the nation at this time without the use of military force.

Someone is leading this and the Lehavim were armed with weaponry they could not have possibly produced themselves. The Lehav people are under constant surveillance, yet the ships they were using had been made with high grade military technology. We need you to make contact with our agent and his people, find out who these conspirators are and report back to us your discoveries."

"Of course," Slydin responded. "We're both ready."

Ciro observed Slydin and Julianne with his pale, glowing eyes. Instantly, the screens before him shifted into view and displayed their bodies under various scans, showing the different anatomical systems at work.

"You say you're ready," Ciro stated, breathing heavily. "Were you ready when your best friend betrayed you? How many more traitors do you have working with you? You will be handling this mission alone."

He turned his head slightly toward Julianne. Ciro's chair arched closer leaning in his direction, until he was positioned several feet away from him.

"Let me make this absolutely clear. The only reason you are being considered for this operation is because Elder Ronne spoke for you. If it were up to me, you would be stripped of your title and exiled from the Federation to the outer rim.

Three-hundred and twenty years ago, I was an Ambassador during the meketric supplicants. When the disease ravaged our system and destroyed nearly one third the entire population, the Federation nearly collapsed, development halted, but we were firm. We led our people, *all* peoples to rebuild. Some of those destroyed in the attacks caused by your negligence, were my descendants. Branches of my family line, that have existed since the Federations inception, have been permanently severed because of *your* oversight."

His statements caught the Captain off-guard and though

his words burned, they were no less true.

"I am sorry for your loss, Ambassador." Slydin replied.

"Sorry?" Ciro mocked, "If you are truly sorry, don't fail the Federation again."

The screens wavered around the area, showing the ship and positioning.

"You will be under heavy scrutiny. Head to the door marked to your left."

A door opened with a red illumination flashing brightly indicating the exit.

"Remember, we are watching you."

His chair turned but his head remained facing the them. Gradually, as Slydin bowed and took his leave, Ciro turned his skull slowly towards the monitors before him. Julianne watched in silence, unsure of what to do. But this was a directive from the Prime Sanctuary.

I must fulfill my duty and redeem my position.

Three Years Ago

The Kitim shuttle was much more compact then the previous vessel. Slydin was situated upright and automatically strapped in as the takeoff commenced.

Ciro's voice broke from an intercom he could not see, but could hear clearly. "You're being drifted through space in one of our satellite repair vehicles. You will arrive shortly at a hub we have stationed above your target. When you arrive, make contact with the manager. Your account number is one fifty-three, seven, five."

Slydin thought to himself for a while. The manager?

"Okay… can you give me further details? Anything…"

The satellite sped through space. There wasn't much time to comprehend what was going to happen. The boarding proceeded quickly and he entered the shuttle to find it powered up and ready.

Slydin consistently repeated the number in his head but confusion set in the moment he stepped out of the transport.

Who was the manager? Where am I going and why was so little detail given? Why am I on Tirat? However, all things considered, their capital Thrace is home to The Economic Universal Trading Operations National Syndicate. This is the banking planet that controls universal monetary policy.

Standing in front of one of the larger banking buildings, Slydin stared calmly at the steady traffic that spread out in the city.

I guess I'm going to see the manager.

Approaching the bank, the doors opened automatically and Slydin felt the cool rush of overworked air conditioning. The inside was a completely open concept and the pristine condition it was kept in made it look like the bank had been built yesterday.

Upon entering the lobby, a group of large, muscular humanoid frames sprouting six arms each stood directly in this path. These impressive beings were the Canaim race from the nation of Tubal. Almost all Federation infrastructure firms were based on their home world. These imposing beings were known to be able to lift almost eight times their massive body weight and remain in prime physical condition throughout their lives. In a matter of weeks, they could refashion barren lands into a prosperous metropolis. An industry that highly serves the Federation as a developmental force that can reshape landscapes and prepare undeveloped nations for technological upgrades.

The group of Canaim were exiting as Slydin arrived. Somehow, despite the enormous lobby, he found himself trying to avoid their oncoming. This brief contact created an awkward pause between them, while trying to figure out an easy way around. The group unanimously looked down at Slydin. The one in the lead gave a soft smile, extended two of his long arms, grasped him by the shoulders with his three thick fingers and held him in place as his cohorts gently passed by. The Canaim before him nodded, released him and then walked on after his friends.

At the counter, an attractive teller greeted Slydin who quickly asked for the manager. She pressed a button under her workspace and smiled. "He will be here in one moment, Sir."

A well-dressed man younger than Slydin, arrived. Leaning in close and speaking in calm tones, Slydin began, "I would like to review my account. One fifty-three, seven, five."

He leaned back, looked over the Captains' shoulder and then smiled. "We have to meet in the back for that. I will be right over."

As he rounded the desk, Slydin looked over his shoulder, wondering what the manager was looking at. As he trailed behind him, all the doors leading to their destination opened mechanically. It was a smooth transition from the spacious lobby into a tight office.

He invited Slydin to sit at his desk. Slydin was completely unsure of what he was supposed to do or say.

Am I taking out money? Making a deposit? After the account number, Ciro gave me no other information.

An awkward silence set in and lasted longer than either of them were used to. All he did was stare until the manager finally broke the tension.

"You're Captain Slydin of the Jericho, aren't you?"

He nodded, still not exactly sure what was going on or what would happen next.

"Of all people to send… I'm Wil. The bank manager."

The two shook hands as Slydin wondered if this was some strange joke Ciro had played on him. Wil retrieved a small folder, removing a handful of papers which he placed neatly across the desk, nodded and slid the rest of the folder towards him.

"There it is," he said proudly. "We have all the names and locations."

Most of the charts presented were purchase orders and

invoices. Slydin carefully looked them over, but while trying to read the numbers listed in small print his vision went blurry and he looked up at Wil for some help.

"You have no idea why you're here, do you?" Wil asked.

"I have some idea," he responded trying to sound at least slightly less ignorant.

"It's not surprising," Wil explained. "Things have become… risky. These are some of the greater accounts of Meschech, the corporate system… we are being watched. Not in a direct way, but our syndicate has been compromised. It's all there in detail."

He stared intently at Wil and then at the file. He browsed the pages, then set it aside and leaned closer to the bank manager.

"I want you to pretend that I understand nothing you just said. Explain this to me like I'm a box and make everything fit."

Wil leaned back, his eyes rolled backward and then nodded quickly. Reassuming his position, he started,

"Recently huge infrastructure projects have been initiated on Casluhim and the surrounding moons. There have been purchases of a lot more material than they need. From the outside things look legitimate. They purchase high grade metals for housing projects and low-grade metals for their upgrades. In reality, this excess has been used to create multiple fleets and a large arsenal to arm the Lehavim and probably other groups."

"Why wouldn't the Federation be alerted?" Slydin asked skeptically. "They have a multi-planetary leadership panel. How could their senate approve this?"

"Most of the senate members had their accounts cleared months ago," stated Wil abruptly.

Slydin stared at him, hoping he would continue his simplistic explanation.

"…The leadership of the Plishtim nation is dead."

His statement sent a shock through his body. *How? An entire ruling body? How could this be at all possible without Federation knowledge?*

Slydin now suspected that the cyborg, the banker and even the Elders were paranoid.

"It's a movement, Slydin. A Secessionist movement. The attacks on Hellas and Reu have been a well-placed distraction. Even the refugee crisis has been used by them. It has spread thin the military and divided the nations. When they need access to specialized supplies, like on Tarshish, they raid. It's claimed to be a criminal incident."

It unnerved him that they knew about Tarshish, but what he said was true. The Federation's security force was being overworked.

"How could it possibly happen that a nation's entire leadership would suddenly go missing."

"It's not all of them," Wil replied, "only the ones that did not agree."

"Didn't agree with what?" Slydin countered.

"With whoever is in charge of all this. No one is mentioning any names. We have the bulk of the operation, but the problem we are having is finding the instigator."

"I thought it was Edom. The leader of the Lehavim uprising."

"No," Will retorted. "He was a pawn. A violent, glorified pawn."

"So, what can I do?" he asked. "How do we find out who this *leader* is?"

Wil half-smiled, opening the file that Slydin had cast aside.

"Over one-third of the payments are made in raw materials. Mostly ore-based commodities used for ship production and battery-operated hyperdrive engineering. The only place to get this massive amount of supply is from Patros."

"I know the area," Slydin exclaimed. "I spent over two

years of my diplomatic internship with the nation. But they're not hostile. They don't even have weapons."

A solemn look fell over Wil's face. "They have been placed under a corporate blockade, issued by the nation of Meshchech."

"But that makes no sense," Slydin protested. "They don't have the means for space travel or even use most of our technologies."

"*Someone* does not want us to see what's going on. This is the last piece of the puzzle. We present our evidence tomorrow to the Assembly of Nations. The Elders have been working on this for months and they trust that you can resolve this final issue."

Wil sat back and let him take in everything he had said.

In *all of this, Esav, you were just a tool.*

"I will definitely do this. But why do you need me? Any ambassador can break a diplomatic block"

Wil slid the folder towards him as he rose from his seat.

"Elder Ronne trusts you. Plus, we know for sure you are not corrupt. It's getting hard to tell who's on our side these days."

Picking up the file, Wil led Slydin back to the lobby. After wishing him well, Slydin quickly exited the bank and picked up his intercom, hoping Julianne had returned to the ship.

"Julianne."

"Captain, where have you been? Is everything alright?"

"It's fine," he responded, now disturbed by the insights Wil had brought to his awareness. "I need a pick-up. I'm on Tirat."

"What?! Why are you on Tirat? Never mind, we're coming. Send us your coordinates."

After powering off, his thoughts turned to the nation of Patros. *Have we all been so blind? How could all of this have been going on without us knowing? It doesn't matter now. My mentor is depending on me and I will redeem myself.*

Three Years Ago

Rounding the edge of the inner rim they easily broke the simple corporate blockade with Slydin's Ambassadors' pass and settled within the atmosphere of the small planet of Pathros, where he had spent his final years of diplomatic schooling.

As they were guided into Pathros airspace, the small green planet quickly became a large, encompassing realm of forestry. Colossal hedges, shaped into labyrinthine mazes, could be seen from the air through the ship's windows. Mane brought up viewscreens and displayed the brilliancy of the totally cultivated planet, also allowing the crew to also observe the nation's inhabitants flying over a small stretch of mountains.

"Amazing!" Crimron stated. "I never knew anything in the Federation could be so large."

The ship passed over an enormous forest with trees that were hundreds of feet tall. Slydin thought they might scrape the ship against their tops while gliding onto a makeshift platform, which was just an artificially flat piece of land. Landing softly, Slydin summoned Julianne to his side. With instructions to the crew, the two prepared immediately to disembark.

"Now," he opened to Julianne, "we need to get a record of anything that's been happening here. We will have to work fast as there is no way our presence has gone unnoticed. I have a contact that could help."

While concluding his instructions, the ship began to tremble. "Crimron, hold the engines."

"Captain, the engines are inactive. This is an outside force," he responded.

The viewscreens were also vibrating and were displaying large beings approaching the ship at fast speed. Noticing the stampede, Slydin ordered the crew to remain behind. Motioning to Julianne, they took their leave and upon reaching the planet outside, they felt the tremors and witnessed the advance of the people of Pathros.

There were hordes and Slydin could tell that Julianne was totally unnerved at the presence of such impressive beings. The Patrothim slowed their movement as they neared their position. They surrounded the ship, their bodies sheltering them from the bright sun. Looking up, Slydin gave a loud guttural bellowing. He repeated the process twice more, each time louder than the one before it.

Julianne looked at him as if he had lost his mind, but her surprise faded as one of the locals responded in a similar way.

"What?" he said. "Not all of them speak Federation common."

She continued staring at her Captain like he was a ghost.

"Julianne, meet the stone giants of Pathros."

The gigantic sentient beings all reverberated a loud greeting towards her. Large humanoid formations of rock, some of the smallest being just over twenty feet tall, stood smiling down at them.

One of the giants extended his hand towards Slydin. Stepping onto the grey palm, Slydin was quickly lifted onto his shoulder. Looking down at Julianne he waved, his enthusiasm rising along with the elevation

"Come on Juli, it's actually a lot of fun."

She looked up at Slydin and shouted, but he could barely hear what she was saying. Reluctantly, she stepped onto the hand of another stone giant and like Slydin, was lifted onto his shoulder. Their bodies tended to be ridged and grooved, as if large boulders had been grafted together into the shape of a gigantic anthropoid. The two finally settled within the furrows of the shoulders of their hosts. Gradually, the crowd of giants raced away from the ship. They moved slowly at first, but as the journey progressed, they gained momentum.

The planet seemed to be covered with worked hedges that outgrew even the tallest of their retinue. Everything on the planet was bigger: boasting giant flower beds and huge trees. They passed into a clearing, leaving the gigantic maze and entered a vast landmass made up of flat, cultivated grounds that stretched out before them. It was as Slydin remembered it - regions of farmland.

The massive leaps from the stone giants quickly covered a long stretch of land and they reached a summit where the ground broke into a system of valleys and then a deep can-yon. Stopping at the foot of a mountainous area, the stone giants gently set them down. They bowed and departed.

Julianne, exhilarated by the latest event, looked over at her Captain smiling. "Well, are they going to leave us?"

"No," he responded. "They know we are Ambassadors. Their head-man will be with us soon."

"Head-man? Really?" Julianne teased.

"That's the title," stated Slydin smiling. "I spent years here. This planet's nation had become like a family to me. Those farmlands we crossed, they are the main food production source. They work everything here from the hedge mazes that go on forever to the forests with the trees that stretch so high, their top branches freeze. It is all a product of the stone giants' ingenuity. Even more interesting, their excrement contains many valuable ores: copper, cobalt, gold, indium, manganese and nickel are among the many."

"So then, why is this planet under a corporate blockade?" Julianne asked.

"Well, it seems obvious, most of the ores produced here are essential in the production of different communication and battery systems for interplanetary travel. No records are ever kept as to how much leaves this planet. The leadership has been made aware of a corporate scheme to create and supply rebel nations with illegal arms. *This* planet and others like it, are being extorted for materials."

Julianne's face contorted slightly as she thought about the situation. Theories spun around in his head about the events that had unfolded.

There was a lot of forethought put into this. A conspiracy that involved more than simple blood lust and piracy. How many more nations have fallen victim to this and why has the Federation been so blind?

Great tremors shook them from their thoughts. At once, Julianne darted towards Slydin. It looked like the far mountainside began to walk and with every step, seemed to shake the earth surrounding them. Slydin was looking up and smiling as a massive giant settled into a sitting position, leaning against the gradient. Its large head turned toward them at an angle as it stared down at them.

"I think you've lost weight," he shouted. The stone giant smiled in response.

"Slyyydin, it has been too long."

"He's a lot bigger than the others," Julianne added.

"Yeah, the ones who brought us were actually quite small," admitted Slydin who proceeded toward his old friend and sat on his foot, beckoning Julianne to follow.

"Thoures, I'm sorry for not visiting sooner," opened Slydin.

He slouched forward, covering the two with his immense shadow.

"I would have loved to see you sooner. You... You could have met my son."

"Your son!" Slydin was dumbstruck by the news. The giants breed only in their later years and even then, it is a slow process. "That's great! Thoures, I..." his initial excitement was quickly cut down by his friend's downcast appearance.

"Thoures, what's wrong? What's been happening here?"

His head bobbed side to side as he tried to articulate his thoughts. Thin rivers ran down his sculpted jawline as he explained the situation.

"They took him... I could do nothing. Even with all my strength... I wasn't strong enough to save him. My only boy."

"Thoures, I need you to speak to me." Slydin activated his transmission brace and connected with the Federation overseers. "You need to tell us everything. We will help you."

Thoures met his friends' gaze, now at least somewhat reassured, he began in a slow, dejected manner.

"My son is barely old enough to stand past my knees. We were working the fields when they came. They flew in strange ships that spouted a fog wherever they sailed."

Slydin locked eyes with Julianne, whose eyes spoke what they were both thinking.

"Those ships," she whispered, "are definitely Plishtim tech."

"When they landed, they attacked us," Thoures continued. "Most weapons cannot harm my people, but these were powerful. We fought them back and destroyed many of the attackers, but they had used our defense as a distraction. They chained my son and took off with him."

Even though hearing this story from his friend, he found it hard to believe. Who would be fool enough to attack the stone giants? Most Federation weapons outside of a bombardment would barely affect them.

"Thoures, tell me," Slydin interjected, "how is it possible to even carry any of you off this planet? You would need a large bulk cruiser."

The giant seemed to be deliberating to himself about it for a while. Slydin knew very well that he had little to no understanding of technology. Even imagining a vessel big enough to house them and then take off was almost beyond his own comprehension.

"I had never seen one like it. It was not like the ones that deliver the ground nourishments. It seemed to be made to hold him. They took him and then said to us that they would return him so long as we delivered our natural products to them. If we tell anyone, or hold back on deliveries... they said they would kill him."

Slydin paused for a moment. These acts of thievery, even after all these years in the Federation, were completely foreign to him. The giants shared everything in common and never met with any other nation in an adversarial manner.

"Who could we call?" Thoures asked, now disgruntled. "We do not have any such means to make use of the tools that most nations have. Slydin, what did we do? Why would they take my son?"

Thoures' eyes teared again, his confusion and sadness overwhelming him. Slydin interrupted his thoughts, trying to get more information for the mission.

"Thoures... Thoures listen, I need you to tell me about the attackers."

"Slydin, I always believed I had strong hands," his tone became even more discordant. His soul was tortured by the reenactment of the events. "Slydin, I fought them, but I could not save my son. Whenever they arrive for materials, I ask them when he will be returned..."

"Thoures, please. Please, tell me about the attackers."

He breathed in deeply and slowly articulated his speech. Stone giants had a slower cognitive function than most of the races.

"They looked much like the manner of your people, but they wore strange face plates. I could not see them."

It was definitely Plishtim.

"Okay. We have enough for now. Thoures, we are going to find your son. I am so sorry for not seeing you sooner, old friend."

His face lit up as Slydin touched his shin. *This is enough,* Slydin thought, incensed. *The Federation had endured this torment of hidden agendas and secretive allegiances long enough. Today, all of this will end.* He knew the council's vengeance would be swift.

A small group of the Federation's council were listening to the conversation, led by Elder Philo. He opened a line of communication with Slydin, to initiate countermeasures. "We have now absolute proof of the Casluhim's treachery. I propose full military action and a complete bombardment of the planet and its surrounding moons. All place your votes now."

There was a moment's pause.

"Good," Elder Philo affirmed. "Place an emergency close on all warp doors. Send word to the AshKenaz hauling unions that they are to board their nearest landing areas and make room for the military offensive. Tell the fleets of Gomer and Sidon to get into position and prepare for a bombardment of the Casluhim nation, starting with their moon Caphtor. Send out a warning and then jam all inter-planetary communications. Slydin, do you copy?"

"Yes, Sir," Slydin replied.

"Call up your ship and join the offensive. When we are finished, you must make contact with the remaining leadership of the Plishtim," added the Elder.

"Understood, Sir. However, if you like, I can make contact with some of the Ambassadors I know in the area. Maybe we can encourage some to surrender before the fighting becomes fierce," I countered.

"Very well," the Elder agreed. "Do it quickly. We'll keep our transmission open."

Julianne called to the Jericho. After Slydin reassured Thoures that his son would be their first priority, the ship arrived. They swiftly boarded and set out to the nation of Casluhim, home of the Plishtim peoples.

"Captain," Crimron informed, "we are approaching the Caphtor atmosphere.

"Good, now open a channel and contact ambassador 80-30-300-400-10-40"

It took a while, but the response came and a masked figure with glaring, black eyes and dark, thick, tentacle-like hair appeared on the screen. His voice sounded low, dark and metallic, as was the nature of the Plishtim. Their vocals were always obscured by the masks they wore.

"Captain Slydin, it has been a long time."

"Golates! I am pleased to see you alive! We understand your nation has been undergoing a restructuring. We need your help to avoid as many civilian casualties as possible. I know your people have been through a lot..."

"No Slydin, I don't think you fully comprehend the situation *you* are in. You know, you almost succeeded. If the Elders had just worked closer with the nations they ruled, you could have prevented all of this." His blunt interruption signified the worst of Slydin's fears.

"Golates, whatever they've done, I know you and many of the others were forced against their will..."

His laughter pierced through the bridge. "Against our will? The only *will* we lost was our own! At that academy, where those mind readers brainwashed us; where we became convinced that our nations should become slaves to one another and fall under Federation rule!"

"You cannot be serious. We were raised together at the academy! That was our home! How can you say this?" Slydin pleaded.

"Home!?" Golates shouted. "We were taken from our homes. We were robbed of our youth and convinced that submission to some ancient authority would give meaning to our lives. My people have lived under the subjugation of the Federation. My nation has been forced to produce goods for the rest of the system. I witnessed children working in factories to meet the Federation's production quotas. Where were you!? Where was the Federation?"

"Whatever the problems are, we can work them out. We are *brothers,* Golates. This is madness, how can you support this?"

"Support? You still don't get it. There is no working this out. Not anymore. I have purged my head of the illness those mind-bending fiends forced onto us," he admitted proudly.

What he was saying about their mentors ripped into Slydin and his irritation turned to anger. "The only *illness* you have is the one you are inviting for your people with this rebellion."

"You see," he continued, "they instilled us with a Federation arrogance. They force our nations into a synthetic cooperation and demand that we all work as one. If we decide to any sort of individual enterprise, we are cut off and starved until we comply. *Those* are Federation ideals."

"When we completed our training," Slydin started, "we swore an oath to serve the nations. To keep things together, as one. Those are the true Federation ideals and they are your ideals," he reaffirmed. "And we made our promise to uphold those laws. You won't be allowed to abandon your duty without punishment."

Golates laughed at this last remark. "Slydin, I want you to see something."

The screen turned and the young stone giant appeared in view. He was chained and frightened. His head darted in many directions. Slydin could not see any other Plishtim, but he knew they had him surrounded.

The Plishtim entered the area and dragged the chains holding his arms forward, securing the young giant. His voice not developed like his fathers sounded more like a distressed honk. The young one fought back against his assailants. He struck down many at a time and broke free of his chains. The screen was thrust off target and Golates could be heard ordering his restraint. When he refocused the transmission feed, another Plishtim had brought a large drill with a hand crank. He began to wind the machine and it spewed out smoke as it charged with life.

Slydin could hardly believe his eyes. It was him all along. The attack on Hellas, the weapons supply to the Lehavim, Esav and now… *this*.

"Stop, Golates!" he ordered. "You're beyond this. Let the child go. I will give myself and my ship as a hostage in his place."

Golates turned to the monitor, "How noble. I gave my word if his father didn't speak to anyone about our dealings, he would have his son back." He gestured to the Plishtim who edged forward with the drill toward the head of the young stone giant. It honked loudly and sporadically. Slydin understood the language clearly. He was calling to his father.

"Golates, stop! Let me take his place!" Slydin yelled.

The young giant's head tilted back at the drills approach until its natural biology prevented it from leaning any further. The drill slowly entered his skull and at first, his face shook and contorted. As the drill drove deeper, his young head shuddered violently until the machine paused, holding the young giant in place. The drill reversed and slid out smoothly, dropping the giant to the floor with a loud crash.

Slydin's body was overcome with shock. Words would not surface. His thoughts and vision blurred. The crew were also horrified at the sight.

"Slydin, look at him. *You* did this to him. Your failure did this. I'm going to drop his body back onto Pathros and show the nation what a Federation promise looks like."

The transmission was cut and the screen went black. The

bridge was silent. Mane quickly interrupted. "Captain, we have movement from hostiles moving into attack position."

How could I let this happen? What will I say to Thoures? He just lost his son and I couldn't do anything.

"Sir," Mane started, "we have to move. There is a massive influx of Plishtim fighters rising from Caphtor."

The scanners filled with activity. Golates was not the leader of a terrorist organization, but the commander of legions. Thousands of fighters took to the skies and prepared for an attack. The fleets of Gomer and Sidon reinforced their position as a transmission from Jandin came through.

Slydin couldn't hear anything. His heart was racing from shock and as he could feel the beads of sweat accumulating and then pouring down his face.

"Captain," Julianne called, "we have been asked to relocate behind Federation lines."

Words formed in his head and in his mind, he spoke them to Julianne, but nothing passed his lips.

"Captain," she repeated, now moving to Slydins' side and leaning close, "We need your orders."

All he could do was stare at her in horror. *I had failed so completely, right from the beginning…*

"Slydin," she whispered forcefully, "what do we do?"

…I don't know.

Help... Help, Please Help!

Present Day

"Captain, we have our pathway set," proclaimed Mane. "We will have to make a total of three jumps."

He raised a virtual map and showed the course charted. He enlarged the view of the main jump points and allowed them to cycle automatically, displaying their route with perfect accuracy.

"After the jump, we need to reset our coordinates and launch again. All of it is manual. We need to be in the right place, at the right time, otherwise we may speed into a star or drop too close to a gravitational pull."

Staring at his comrade, Slydin leaned forward in my chair. "And you are sure that your calculations are correct?"

"I checked them with Crimron, Sir," affirmed Mane.

"Alright," he announced, "Let's do this! Everyone strap in. This is still a strange system. We don't know what to expect. Mane, after the third jump, how close to the planet will we be?"

"At the edge of their system, Sir," he replied. "From there, we fly straight in."

After instructing the crew on what to do, they all set to

work. They coasted along a preset pathway mapped out by Crimron and as the time for the jump approached, a countdown sounded. The lights, maps, and screens slowly went out until all that could be seen were some scattered keyboards flickering on the bridge.

Five…Four…Three…

Elder Ronne… I hope you're right about this…

…One…

The ship shot off with powerful force. The upgraded technology was stronger than their ships normal equipment. Everyone was molded uncomfortably into their seats. Slydin's eyes tightened at the increase in pressure. The skin on his face pulled and muscles contorted. His body trembled under the weight of the sudden burst, the ship halted instantly and lightly swayed before settling back into a balanced hovering.

Slydin peeled his arms off the chair, his whole body was aching and the rest of the crew looked to be in the same discomfort.

"Mane… What the hell?" Slydin cried out.

"Sorry Sir," Crimron, asserted. "That was my fault. I didn't factor in for gravitational disturbances."

"Is there any way we can avoid that for next time?" Slydin ordered.

"Well… to be honest… probably not," Crimron replied.

The entire crew now looked uneasy.

"Okay everyone! Brace yourself for round two," Slydin commanded.

"Ugh… hold on, Captain," Mane called out, "we need to recalculate and reposition ourselves. If the crew would like to rest a while, me and Crimron will set up our next jump, Sir."

Everybody settled into their stations as the coordinators continued the preparations. Still recovering from the recent shock, Slydin began to contemplate what they were approaching.

"Captain!" Mane shouted. "I'm getting a transmission."

Turning to Mane, Slydin requested he confirm its source. Slydin and his crew listened intently to the message several times but could not understand what it meant.

"I'll speak with the AshScript," Mane insisted, "to see if it can be translated."

The AshScript took little time in decoding the words. Mane looked at them horrified and went silent. then he issued a command to his virtual console to read the translated message aloud to the bridge.

"Help... Help, please help!"

It repeated over and over.

"Mane, can you find out where it's coming from?" Slydin questioned.

He quickly entered some more commands and a group of bright stars, not far in the distance appeared.

"It's just beyond there, Captain. The radar cannot seem to get past the star's interference."

Without hesitation, he ordered Crimron to speed forward and investigate. The transmission broke for a time but then would repeat.

"Help… Help, please help"

"Can you get a location Mane?" Slydin requested.

"No, Sir. This is strange as it seems to be a repeating broadcast…"

As they soared towards the source, the ship seemed to pick up speed.

"Crimron, slow it down," directed Slydin. "Mane, get us a visual."

Mane brought up a live feed displaying the small group of bright stars. Its light continued to block their visual.

"It won't be long Captain. Once we pass the light stream, we will have a proper view."

The ship sped forward faster. The entire bridge braced themselves at their posts.

"Crimron! Slow it down," Slydin ordered.

"Captain," he returned, "it's not the ship."

What!? Not the ship? Then why are we… looking intently at the screen, he hoped that what he believed to be true would prove false.

Passing out of the glare, Slydin saw for the first time something he thought we would never encounter. A revolution of flowing darkness that circled a black dense center. Silken waves poured towards the midpoint in an elegant cascade. Their ship smoothly drew into the void. His heart raced as he turned and gave orders for an instant retreat.

"It's a black hole! Reverse! Crimron, full power to engines!"

Struggling against the pull of the collapsed star before them, Crimron was sweating as he pushed the steering controls forward all the way. The ship began twisting under the duress of the assailing forces.

All present on the bridge felt the pressure change and many of them began to bleed from the ears as they gripped their consoles. The ship's lights flashed violently and monitors shut down. Mane remained steady, straining against pull. Slydin's body seethed with pain as the supra-natural power of the fallen star weighed in against his biology. It was not long before his cognitive functions ceased and his body went limp. At once, as if in response to their need, the gift of Peleg started up and launched the ship away from what would have been agonizing destruction.

When Slydin awoke, many of the crew members were helping each other to their feet.

He rose to his feet and stretched out, finding it difficult to inhale. The Captain wiped the sweat from his face with a hand smeared in blood. Blood had been pouring from his nose. Slydin felt as if his brain had tried to squeeze out of his skull. A migraine that started in his head now radiated through his whole body. Using the Captain's chair for support, he steadied himself. As things calmed down, Slydin approached Mane.

"Mane," he started, "You're our comm guy right?"

He nodded.

"Why didn't you see the black hole?"

He inhaled with deep raspy breaths, as if each one was to be his last. With the mood Slydin was in, he was definitely about to make that possible.

"I'm sorry," he replied. "I've never actually traced a black hole before and I was so focused on the transmission… it must have been circling. Who knows how long…"

"Mane, listen to me. I don't want any other distractions. Close the damn communication." Slydin felt his anger at the whole situation welling up. "I don't care if Elder Ronne contacts us from whatever *source* he melted into and wants to board. Let's just get to the damn planet!"

He nodded again, lowering his gaze.

"Okay. But, umm… we will need to recharge the boosters and check diagnostics…"

Slydin's gaze cut him off in mid-sentence. The rest of the crew stepped back to their consoles and nursed their wounds.

"Julianne, I'm going to my quarters. Takeover. Call me when we're ready to jump."

Slydin took leave from the bridge as the power returned and the transmission resumed.

"Help… help, please help!"

"Captain," Mane called out. Slydin veered to face him. "Who do you think sent this transmission?"

Looking at the crew as they reset themselves and then back at Mane, Slydin stated the only answer that made any sense, "I don't know, but if we had hesitated, the next message would have been ours."

Slydin left the bridge and headed down the hallway and into his room. Upon entry, he collapsed on the bed and fell into a sea of exhaustion. There were no dreams this time, only a dark black abyss, swallowing his mental perception and easing him into a formless and unconstrained rest.

When Slydin awoke, the blood from his face had dried. He rose slowly, still reeling in pain from the encounter with the black hole. A message from Julianne arrived requesting his presence.

Not eager to keep his compatriots waiting, Slydin headed down the hallway and returned to the bridge. His entrance was slow and deliberate, as he made his way straight to the Captain's chair.

The chair turned and faced him toward a screen showing their flight pattern. Little time was wasted and after a short countdown, they burst through the portal and ended up at the border of a system containing their destination.

Crimron set up the autopilot and Mane scanned for any life or civilizations that could greet them on the way. When they passed the first planet, Mane noted that it was made up mostly of hydrogen and helium. Spanning 200 times the diameter of the planet, large rings circled its massive frame. None of them had ever seen a world with such decoration.

Further on a titan of a planet presented itself with over sixty moons. Everyone watched in silence as Mane scanned for life. Finding none, they passed by, hoping the next planets would be as magnificent as the ones behind.

One other small planet, with a barren wasteland crossed their path. *What possible planet could be nested among such savage environments?* Slydin thought. *Did these worlds collapse of their own? Did their peoples flee to our destination? Were there ever people?*

Seeing nothing but dark space for a long while, Crimron took back control of the ship. He drove them forward at greater speed. Slydin's thoughts drifted again to theories about this system and its planets, a solemn gasp surfaced from the crew looking at the screen, returning him to the present moment.

There... There it is.

All that could be seen was a pale blue point contrasted by the immense depth of space surrounding it.

By the tales he had been fed, Slydin had imagined this planet to have a golden halo beaming out from its orbit with immense traffic from other galaxies arriving for sage advice from the world that was supposed to be a light to all nations. But there was none of that. No satellites or ships. Not even a cautionary transmission. Just a pale blue dot cemented against the darkest space he had ever seen. It was a lonely planet with only one moon.

Was this really our goal?

Slydin commanded Mane to scan the environment. His report confirmed the ecosystem would easily support life.

"All right then," he directed. "Find us a place to land."

Part 3

The Jericho's approach was incredibly unimpressive. The answers to the Federations plight and the universe at large was to be found on this small, blue solitary planet with a single moon orbiting meekly around it's atmosphere.

"We're slowing thrusters Captain," Crimron announced.

"Wait," Slydin interrupted. "Land in an area with easy access to the largest surrounding landmass." After doing some scans over the surface, Slydin pinpointed a perfect location. After sending the map to Crimron the ship's trajectory was adjusted and they sped towards their destination.

"This area is where three great land masses intersect," Slydin stated as they touched down. The ship's power cells cooled as he turned to his crew to set out the plans for the completion of their mission.

"Everyone, listen! Mane, do a scan and find out where the most life is concentrated. Everyone else, pair up. We move in teams to make direct contact with the natives of this planet. Julianne you're with me. Crimron, how fast can our pods reach any given area on this world?"

"Sir, this planet is quite small. We could probably circle it six times within ten minutes," added Mane.

"Good. Our ship is the home base. *Everyone* is required to check in once they've landed and again when any discovery has been made. Also, every ten to fifteen minutes, send a note to the ship confirming your status. Mane will be here to manage your findings and all communications."

Everyone agreed and found their partners. The crew was eager to explore. Looking at Julianne, Slydin led the retreat to the pods. Upon stepping in, he and Julianne noticed the different coordinates on the screen. "Me and Julianne will depart first. Everyone, fall out one at a time. When you arrive at your destination, send word."

The pods rose and took off. The trip did not last long before they had to circle around again.

We actually missed the target? This computer is telling me there were eight billion people here. How can that be? This planet is too damn small.

After finally settling down at the intended area, the two exited the craft and began their observations. Silently, they walked through what once was a colonized area. Large segments of the area were overgrown with weeds and greenery. The buildings, most of which had collapsed, were not spared from the vegetative onslaught.

Slydin turned to Julianne with a thought provoking inquiry. "How long do you think this place has been abandoned?"

She looked back and shrugged.

Carrying on through the urban ruin, they neared an area significantly cooler with a light mist encasing the region. The sound of flowing water was unmistakably heard. It sounded like a deep, raging current. Julianne and Slydin quickened their pace and came to the edge of an overpass. Below was the largest waterfall the two had ever seen.

The cascade stormed downward, in an unending torrent

hundreds of feet below where they stood. Both remained silent, watching and remembering their past together.

"Honestly, I've been dreaming a lot about our days by the waterfalls of Ripath."

"I remember," she stated, not turning away from this massive wonder. "None of them looked like this."

For long stretched-out moments, the falls held a mesmerizing grip on their attention. While drifting into the abstract, Slydin's thoughts turned to his mentor.

Was he wrong about the destination? Were we too late? Are there even beings here at all that can help save our system? What will we do if this endeavor proves to be wrong?

"Captain," a voice over his communicator broke both their reveries. It was Mane.

"Mane, we're here."

"Captain, the others have returned. We've all assembled. We need your report."

"We're on our way."

Julianne nodded, now gripping her upper arms. The apparent cold radiating from the moisture pooling below in great quantities had taken its full effect. Together, they quickly exited without looking behind.

Upon returning to the ship, the other teams had already assembled by the landing area and waited for the Captain before beginning to compile their findings. Viewing his crew, Slydin eagerly awaited their discoveries.

"Okay everyone," he started, "tell me what we know."

The reports were almost unanimous. Every team, no matter which location they surveyed, only reported crumbling cities and a deserted landscape.

Silence now overtook the gathering. Slydin wondered how this whole situation could be any worse.

"Mane," he called out, now running out of ideas. "What are the planetary diagnostics?"

"Well, from what I've gathered using the ships elemental

and property scanners and from the individual scans done by our team's first expedition; its population definitely reached around eight billion and their technology would have been about a millennium ago or so behind our own."

"So, what happened?" I asked.

"Well, I'm not exactly sure. It seems that either a catastrophe or a mass evacuation occurred."

Slydin felt at a loss.

Why did we travel this far? Were the Elders going crazy in their final days? Did they have some sort of mental block? What have I led my crew into? What about all of the events that took us this far? How close we came to death and how much we risked. There must be more. We must be missing something.

"Let's look at what we know. Mass evacuation. When did this happen?"

Crimron stepped forward.

"Not possible. They would not have anything near the technical development to build true spacecraft. We discovered crashed satellites and even mobile transport, most of which was fueled by primitive oils. We ran reconstruction simulations. Captain, this planet at best was incredibly primitive compared to our own nations."

Slydin pieced all of it together silently.

Eight billion people leaving a planet all at once. That is something the Elders would not have missed. Besides, any civilization with the resources to move eight billion people off-planet could definitely colonize an entire galaxy of their own. But while they had resources, they clearly didn't have the tech. What the hell happened here?

"Alright, how about war?"

"No, Sir," responded a crew member. "At the time of departure, there were several wars happening in various parts of the world. Mane sent out a ballistic resonance test early on and we were tasked with the investigation of some of the more active locations. But these were contained. Most places seem unaffected."

"Starvation maybe?" he quickly added.

"No," came Julianne. "Starvation leads to wars."

"It's true," Mane complemented. "The elemental scan revealed segments of fertile land. The scan also showed that in their time, they could have fed their population without a problem."

Slydin's thoughts now drifted to the last possible hope for proving any sort of extermination.

"If it's not any of those, what about widespread disease?"

"We would have found bodies everywhere," a crew member inserted. "Granted, they would have deteriorated, but they would be everywhere. We are talking about eight billion beings."

Common sense had failed Slydin and his crew.

"How do billions of people, with a well-established but low-tech civilization, just suddenly disappear?"

The crew went silent, hoping that someone among the ranks would have an answer, or even an idea.

Mane broke in against the silence. "Well, we did find out what they looked like."

"Yes, captain," stated one of the diagnostic team excitedly. "We found many graveyards. Not mass graves or anything, just ordered burial sites. We did a refractor-metric scan of the area and discovered entire body samples."

She displayed a virtual screen from her wrist band showing the skeletal reconstruction of many different bodies.

"Also," she added, "we found this."

The next display was as impressive as the great waterfalls: Four gigantic faces carved into the side of a mountain. It looked like something out of a legend.

Their faces… they look like us! Slydin thought.

Mane spoke in on the subject, "Captain, this race of beings did not look so different from us. Sentient by nature and developed under similar conditions to our evolution."

Assessing the situation, Slydin decided to be proactive.

"Their technology - if they evolved like us, then they developed like us. You said it was similar to ours. We need to find any sort of mass storage drives. Did anyone return with samples?"

Some of the crew members presented small flat deteriorated devices from their scouting.

"These," one stated, "are portable communication devices. They would have been operational at the time but this planet's communication system has been down for thousands of years. Also, every sample we found is severely degraded."

"New plan," he announced to the crew, whose attention to any strategy that could put them ahead was overwhelmingly welcomed. "Mane, do a specialized scan. Find us any locations of technological presence. We need to know what happened here and what may be left for us in regard to our mission."

Mane jumped into action, returning to the bridge where he set to work. Then, Slydin turned his attention to the others.

"Everyone, keep to your teams. Each of you will get a location. When you arrive on site, gather any and all technical devices that may have valuable information stored on them. We need this badly, so be thorough."

Mane's coordinates were sent to the crew. Each pair studied their locations and returned to their pods. Slydin interrupted Crimron and told his partner to take this mission solo. After they had all left and no one was within hearing distance, he gestured to Crimron.

"Do we have enough power to take us back to the Federation?"

"Captain," Crimron began, "what are you talking about?"

"This mission is obviously a failure. Whatever the Elders were looking for has been gone for a long time. The Elders were melting away when they gave these instructions and were clearly mistaken."

Crimron went silent. It was way out of character to question an Elder. Their knowledge was always so precise that obedience was typically the most logical response to their mandates.

"Do we have enough power, Crimron?"

He was clearly uncomfortable at the idea of an Elder being wrong. The entirety of their lives and the very existence of the Federation was held together by their counsel. Crimron looked back at him.

"Honestly, we may be able to make it to the edge of this galaxy. But not further."

Slydin's heart sank.

I have failed as an ambassador and now I am the only Captain in the history of the Federation to strand his crew on an abandoned planet.

Thoughts of Slydin's many unmitigated failures flooded his mind. Quietly, he headed towards the ship to go rest in his quarters.

"Captain," Crimron called out, "what about the results from the teams?"

He spun violently.

"What results? There won't be any! Whatever happened on this place happened thousands of years ago? Even *if* we find something that isn't corrupted, the best it can be is a storage of this nation's current day knowledge, which by the way, excludes interstellar power cell animation."

Crimron now understood. The entire scouting mission was a ruse to distract the crew while Slydin tried to salvage what was left of their excursion.

"Umm… Captain," Mane interrupted. "You know, the Elders used to communicate with the planets of the Federation. We can probably do the same here."

"With the letters, you mean?" he questioned. "They can do that?"

"No. Not the letters themselves. We have a Child of Diklah onboard. Once he is planted and interacts with the environment, we can communicate with him."

It was brilliant, Slydin thought.

The Elders would always start at the heart of the nation and use their influence to persuade the very attitudes and hidden forces of the planets before addressing the nation's citizens.

"How did you come up with this?" Slydin asked, now intrigued.

"Well, it wasn't me. The child has wanted to come out since we landed. He said it was imperative to his task so that his people may live on."

Slydin's intrigue died and his irritation rose.

"Mane… why haven't you said anything? I could have held off the second search."

Mane thought about it for a moment. "No one really asked me and I was preoccupied with your commands for the scouting missions."

There is no Federation law out here. I could just kill him.

"Go get the child and plant him out here." Slydin's aggravated tone betrayed his inner resolve. *I swear he does this shit on purpose.*

Julianne emerged with the child, holding most of its vines together. Mane raised it from its home in the makeshift plant stand and its roots shot towards the ground. The Child's entire vegetal composition immediately shifted while its vines blossomed and spread throughout the new setting. After a few minutes, Slydin asked Mane to question the Child.

"Not yet, Captain. While we were aboard the ship, the plant and I had many talks. It will be a little while before he is ready for communication with the heart of the world."

Slydin was staring at the plant now resting in its new habitat and then looking towards Mane, obviously enthralled at the plant child's enjoyment. How could a Communications Officer possess such a high proficiency be totally offset by a stunning lack of social skills?

"How long until we can get answers?" Slydin queried.

"He'll tell us," Mane responded.

When the crew returned to the ship, they had, as expected, very little by way of any of this planet's devices. What they did bring had not been used for thousands of years and none of the components worked properly.

With nothing left to do but wait, Slydin gave orders for the crew to retire. Night was advancing and after surveying the unfamiliar stars revealed by the darkened sky, everyone took to their chambers, leaving Diklah's exiled offspring to discover what they had exhausted themselves over. Slydin fell into the deepest sleep of his life, he slept until morning, without dreaming or disturbance.

"Captain," came a voice in the distance. Slydin rocked his head slightly, hoping to ignore the request.

"Captain," the voice said again.

"Maybe we should leave him alone?"

Yes, yes, leave him alone, please... begged Slydin, still mostly asleep and desperately wanting to remain that way.

Julianne broke into his chambers and woke Slydin violently. "Captain, your presence is required."

Rising, still tired and bothered by the sudden intrusion, he followed Julianne out of the craft and stood in shock.

How could this have happened? I never would have guessed anything like this would be possible.

It stretched out for miles. All around the ship and spanning far beyond where Slydin could see, the Child of Diklah had grown into a massive garden that now enveloped the area surrounding the ship. Most of the crew were eating the fruit produced by this growth spurt.

"It looks like even if we are stuck here, at least we'll have lots to eat," stated Julianne.

Slydin remained fixed on the widespread vegetation around him.

I think I greatly underestimated this child's nation. If we can even call him a child any longer…

"Captain," Mane shouted, interrupting his thoughts. Slydin turned to him.

"It's like a garden," Mane opened, "now that he has soil he can produce many kinds of the foods that we will need to survive. We've been talking all morning and due to our aid in preserving his nation, he has taken it upon himself to safeguard us. He will spread throughout the planet if he needs to."

"Can he speak with the heart of the planet?" I asked.

"Absolutely," Mane assured.

The crew were sampling the produce yielded by their vegetal companion as he followed Mane into the center of the large garden. At an isolated spot, Mane sat down with Slydin.

"Now," Mane began, "we could technically talk anywhere. But I like this area *best*."

"What happened here?" Slydin asked.

Mane launched a virtual tab from his wrist and using the Bavel letters as an interface, began to receive the message.

"You have to be more specific, Captain," he stated.

"Sure, what happened to the inhabitants of this world?"

Mane looked down allowing the letters to permute and

shift on his screen.

"He says… they're in heaven?"

"Mane, what the hell does that mean?"

"Try another question Captain," he insisted.

"What is heaven? Where is it? What are you talking about?"

A moment of pause followed. "Well…" Mane replied slowly, "they are definitely not dead. That's all he's saying."

Slydin glared at Mane who shrugged defensively gesturing to the screen indicating all he could do was read the messages presented.

"Okay, then…" Slydin thought carefully before his next question. "Where is heaven?"

Mane looked quickly towards his screen. "Outside."

Standing up in frustration, Slydin began walking back towards the ship. Mane followed behind trying to catch up. Even speaking with him had pulled at Slydin's last nerve. Entering the ship, Slydin made his way to the bridge to continue scanning with Mane trailing behind.

"Captain, I really think we need to try and understand this more."

Rubbing his eyes, Slydin met his gaze. "Mane, I'm tired. We're on a strange planet far from home. We have no way of returning and the best we've accomplished is minor telepathy and a sustainable food supply."

"Captain, I think it's more than that," Mane quickly countered. "It's true the words are archaic, but that's because these beings see things differently than we do. He says that they are outside. Do you think it's possible that the people we are here for never left?"

A profound stillness brought on by Mane's assertion immobilized the Captain. *If they are not gone… then where?*

"Mane, go out and check on the crew," he said softly.

Mane nodded and Slydin retreated to his chambers. On the way, he gathered the tome from Bavel. Reclining on his bed, he examined the book to find the letters moving in sequence, appearing to be joyful.

I know you can connect to anything we are able to interact with. I need your help to speak with something... outside.

Slydin stared for hours as the letters permuted. He tried communicating with the growing plant life and only received enigmatic responses. Nothing was working. Exhausted, he leaned back in bed letting his weariness turn to rest with sleep arriving shortly after.

. . . .

Slydin walked outside, he was alone as the sun rose, casting a mild haze over the now immense garden. He squinted to focus his vision.

What's wrong with my eyesight? Is this a side effect from the environment of this world? Where is the crew?

Investigating the area, he called out to Julianne. Relief came quickly as he heard movement from behind. Upon turning, the sudden shock dispelled any reassurance he had felt the moment before.

A large ramp of light, like a dense beam from a bright sun, extended on a slant upwards past his line of sight. Looking to see its source, it became difficult to tell if it was radiating from the sky or emerging from the earth. Slydin observed the phenomena and noticed that the ramp was filled with activity. Humanoid bodies of light were traveling, some moving upwards and some down. He looked behind toward the ship, hoping to see someone from his crew. As his head swung back, the beings halted and their attention focused on him.

"Who are you?" he asked.

Silence…

"Are you from this planet?"

Their response came as one, but Slydin noticed no mouths moving. Their faces remained motionless.

"We are One. We live in the Upper Force."

Slydin was unsure how to respond, yet his desire for answers pushed him to continue.

"We have been looking for you…" he paused, now searching for the crew. "Why can't we see you? How do we speak with you?"

The AshScript now flowed through the ramp in streams. Individual letters were absorbed into the sentient beings which then appeared burned into their foreheads. When it seemed as if all of them had a sign personally inscribed, they looked towards him.

"You are standing at the gate of heaven…"

Suddenly, he was surrounded by them. Slydin could not see anything past their forms, other than the fiery letters inscribed into their heads.

"Gather together at the gate of heaven. You have all the keys…"

… Slydin jolted awake, shaking and sweating. It took a while to focus and call to mind the recent dream which was slowly leaving his memory. Sitting up, he noticed the AshScript had smothered his chambers with a repeated verse streaming over the walls. Slowly, he stood, taking the tome of Bavel.

We have been doing this wrong. Since the beginning, we have done all of it wrong. Everything was wrong.

Summoning the crew, he ordered all personnel to meet him outside. The letters swarmed over his body and returned to the book. He left the ship where most of the crew were already waiting and as the final members emerged, words failed him. Despite his deepened insight, he had no idea what he was supposed to say.

The crew gathered before Slydin as he stood holding the aged tome of Bavel. With everyone's attention settled on their Captain, he spoke up.

"Mane. You were right. What we are looking for is here. However, how we are looking for it is completely wrong. We will never complete our mission if we continue to search the way we have."

"Captain, what do you suggest?" Crimron asked.

Slydin, trying to make sure his next words were carefully thought out. *Either this will work out perfectly, or I really am crazy.*

Slowly, they made their way to a comfortable location not far from the ship but in the sight of the immense garden that had now spread even further into the horizon. Many of the crew members silently glanced over at Julianne trying to understand the situation. She could only respond with half-shrugging, apologetic looks.

After the initial confusion, everyone instinctively formed

a circle and sat quietly, awaiting the next moments which could very well prove their Captain's mental instability. Slydin gently opened the Bavel tome, letting the AshScript swarm over the ground. They spread forth in a chaotic sweep and then began to spiral, imitating the crew's seating pattern.

Their spinning slowed until one letter remained in front of each crew member. At first there was an awkward waiting. Everyone became unsure as to what was happening. Some of the crew prepared to speak but held back, not wanting to break the silence. They stared at the letters, then at each other... Mane cleared his throat to interrupt, when the AshScript shot towards each crew member.

The shock of how fast it happened left Slydin's vision blurry. He pressed his fingers against his forehead to ease the sudden tension. When his eyesight realigned, he shot backwards from his seated position, landing on the ground as now visible, standing before him, was one of the sentient beings from his dreams, holding its finger out towards him. In a state of panic, he rapidly scurried backwards as his thoughts immediately turned to his crew. His head spun trying to catch a glimpse of his comrades.

He was instantly calmed when he heard Julianne call out to him.

"Captain."

Julianne's voice had a stunning degree of concern. "Are you hurt?"

Slydin finally noticed a single letter from the AshScript cemented on her head. He took a moment and stared at her.

She's looking at me, worried and not noticing this other... guy over here. She can't see him. Even when I'm right I look crazy.

"Okay, so I don't think you're here to harm us," he stated openly, now confusing the crew even more. "Is anyone hurt?"

They all looked at each other as Mane began to assess the obvious.

"Well. Ugh. We have AshScript on our faces now. But I think everyone is fine. Except of course… *you?*"

Thanks Mane. I always look forward to your reports, thought Slydin.

"Everyone, back into the circle," ordered Slydin.

The crew quickly responded. Once the circle was formed, Slydin cautiously joined their ranks. Not sure what to do next, Slydin analyzed the situation trying to make sense or find some logic in all that had happened. He could still see the being. Slydin tried to see if it was an ocular hallucination or worse, if he was still dreaming.

Tired of trying to figure it all out, he took a direct approach, "Alright. You're up. Where are we? Who are you? What do we do now?"

The crew were now totally perplexed as Slydin awaited a response.

"We live in an Upper Force!"

Instantly, his whole body was seized in pain. He dropped to the ground. The entire crew fell alongside him, writhing in agony. The AshScript on their foreheads had turned a bright red and discharged a torturous burning.

"We are pure intellect. You and your friends have evolved to become our exact opposite."

The voice sounded like thunder hammering Slydin's mind. Surges of pain teemed throughout his body. Looking towards Julianne his vision distorted with every word.

"You have reached a state where you must unify with us to reach the Upper Force."

. . . .

Slydin's breathing was labored as he rose to consciousness.

How long was I out? Julianne…? What happened?

Slydin slowly rose to his feet. The entire crew were in the same condition as Slydin and many struggled to help each other. Large vines spread out before the mentally wounded, the native of Diklah began to offer food to help the ailing crew members.

Slydin could feel the remnant spasms from his first contact surge through his body. Everyone looked terrible. The letters had departed from their foreheads. Crimron and a crew member helped Mane to his feet and Julianne staggered towards him. She was sweating and shaking. She almost collapsed on her approach but managed to face him and ask the question on everyone's mind.

"Slydin, what the hell was that!?"

With the crew now calmed, all eyes moved towards their Captain. He had no answers for why this happened, but he did understand.

"This is the reason why we're here."

"The food helps a lot," Julianne said as she ate from the produce of a nearby vine. "It seems to encourage a faster recovery."

"I don't think that's a coincidence," Crimron pointed out.

"You're right," Slydin added, while eating alongside his comrades who were still in shock from the first contact. "Nothing about our mission has been an accident." The crew looked at him unsure of what to make of his comment as he continued to eat. Silently, they begged him for more of an explanation, but there was nothing more to say.

I will make contact again, thought Slydin. Rising quickly, he addressed Julianne, "Listen, while I'm away, you're in charge."

Slydin swiftly raised his hand cutting off her typical objection. "My comm-link will be temporarily powered down. Stay by the ship. I will not be gone long."

A slight breeze swept over his face as he toured the familiar scenery. Slydin moved deeper into the garden away from the ship. As he travelled, his thoughts raced.

Where are you? How can there be so many of you yet I sense nothing? If everything has a purpose, then why is this one so unclear?

"Why can't I just speak with you?" complained Slydin. "What could any of this mystery and pain possibly achieve?"

He waited for a response… and waited still longer…

I am an ambassador. It makes sense that I was sent but why can't I talk to them? The vines stretched over to his side offering some new grape-like offshoots to eat.

"Thank you, friend," Slydin said taking the food gratefully. Upon sitting down and consuming the grapes, he noticed the taste was nothing like that of a fruit.

This tastes like cake!

As he continued to eat, AshScript swarmed over the ground accumulating together in a serpentine form, surrounding his location. Slydin tapped the controls on his wrist opening a virtual screen. The letters settled atop and began to shift allowing clear communication with the garden.

"I have been given permission to cover this world and provide for its inhabitants. The sustenance I give will bestow a taste differently to whoever eats it. I hope this meets with your approval."

He almost choked trying to respond.

"Yes! Yes, very much so," Slydin responded.

"It seems like you are full now. You must get up and follow my paths. They are waiting for you," the child instructed.

"What…?"

The thick layers of greenery loosened, clearing a straight narrow path for him to follow. Jumping to his feet, Slydin walked as the path formed in front of him. Moving forward, the vegetation closed behind while he stepped through. Unaware of his location, Slydin persisted. His pace quickened as the prospect of what could be behind the next clearing cemented a blind reasoning within him, lifting him above any doubts.

Much time passed, yet his speed never faltered. *What is all this for? If this is the mission, I want it finished. I will reach the end. But what am I moving towards?*

The ground now took a steep rise and Slydin's speed slowed, while struggling to adapt to the uphill climb. The garden was now very dense and despite the vegetation parting, he could not see beyond the botanical shroud. Even feeling the resistance and pain in his legs, he rushed onward. Sweat poured from his face as his heart beat wildly.

I don't care if I die here. Just let me finish what I started. I owe that much to Elder Ronne.

The garden had ceased its path-making and Slydin struck hard against a wall made of plant life. With his surroundings now stationary and his destination assured, Slydin quickly calmed. He did a full turn observing the vegetation that now encased him. Opening the virtual screen on his wrist, he read the AshScript.

We are here.

"Okay. So, what is *here?*" *I'm surrounded entirely by the garden. How far has it actually spread?*

As if in tune with his thinking, the miles of bush lowered themselves, giving the Captain a spectacular view from the high point which he now stood at. The garden encompassed the entire foreground. The Child of Diklah had revitalized the area. It looked as if the whole planet would eventually be consumed by its expansion.

We are atop a hill; with all this greenery, I can't even see the ship.

Breaking away from the majestic scenery, Slydin looked to the AshScript on his screen.

"I have spread myself through great spans and after the rains, I will spread even further."

The rains? Looking up for the first time, Slydin noticed clouds forming. Turning himself from the distraction, he returned his focus to the task at hand.

"Alright, I'm here. Now what?" he waited… "My world is in danger. The lives of so many have already been lost…"

"There are many worlds," came an inner voice, congruent with the AshScript on the screen, *"but only one life."*

Not understanding, Slydin kept calm. *It doesn't matter what I think or know. I'm here and if I'm going to learn, they will have to teach me.*
"We need your help. Please, I'll do anything you ask."

"What you've been seeking is here. You must unify with the Upper Force we all live in."

Slydin stared at the garden around him.
I heard this before. What do I do now? I barely understood anything up to this point. I wish I could see…
"Show me."

A single AshScript from the screen began to glow a bright red. It detached from its place and raced up Slydin's arm to his forehead. Before Slydin could react, it burned into his skin causing a searing, overwhelming pain throughout his body. His vision distorted and he nearly collapsed. As his perception returned to normal, Slydin steadied his balance, rubbing the mark on his brow. Encircling him again, as before, were thousands of humanoid beings. This time, he faced them without fear.

"The Upper Force has created the entire universe opposite itself. This ensures development to a point where we reveal the truth about the nature of reality: it is completely self-seeking and inevitably destroys itself."

Slydin listened as the beings seemingly spoke as one. Their

voices sounded like the rush of thunderous waves. His legs barely supported his body and he struggled to force himself to remain standing.

"We will disclose this hidden reality. Continue to hear our words and you will transform into what you were destined to be since the beginning of creation."

This wasn't what Slydin expected. He couldn't make sense of anything these beings were saying. Besides the reverberation of their voices causing him physical harm, what they were claiming only added to a list of questions that seemed to grow exponentially as their conversation progressed. Despite the pain, thoughts surfaced of his mother, his mentor and his crew. He had to take control of the dialog if he was going to understand his situation.

"How is it you came to be the way that you are?"

"We suffered immensely before turning towards the proper way. Our race did not always live as we do now, and as a result of wars, famines and extreme conflict we were forced to radically change our way of being or become extinct. This led to our redemption."

Slydin began to comprehend the magnitude of what had happened to this world. The federation and its nations were not merely meant to be repaired by some secret formula or wise advice. The solution was a revolutionary change so complete that the core of their being would surpass their ingrained hostility. All at once his fear subsided. He needed to know more. Recalling their first contact through the Child of Diklah, new questions burned in his mind.

"Heaven. You said before… our friend said before, that you were in heaven. Is that the name of your nation? Is this the planet we are on?"

"Before our correction, we measured reality by what we could sense. This produced a state of being that was selfish and completely self-absorbed. Heaven is what completes our perception, allowing us to achieve a deep connection with one another and a unity with the Source."

Now, Slydin became absorbed by what he heard. Along this unfamiliar path leading to an unknown destination, a single word brought to mind the words of his beloved mentor.

The Source. Elder Ronne had taught me about this, Slydin thought, but it was always so transcendent. There was never anything tangible that I could prove about The Source. His race's telepathic abilities allowed access to a higher plane of thinking, which left the rest of us stranded behind them. In times of great need, they would contact this "Source."

Slydin began to wish he had paid more attention to his teacher's lessons on the abstract forces that the universe concealed. If something was beyond his understanding he would dismiss it as unimportant. But everyone did that. No matter how strong or advanced the civilization might be, they had always differed from the Elders.

They led us in everything and their advice saved us from countless catastrophes. But we were always following. We could never sense this Source for ourselves and when the Elders were gone, our Federation's unity died with them.

"Where is the Source? Why can't we see it?"

We all stand opposite to its form. We cannot detect it unless the ability is imparted to us. It is the cause of all creation, the root of all emotion, the heart of the collective soul. All beings, at every level, is sustained and governed by this ultimate giving force.

Slydin swallowed deeply, not exactly sure what to make of the last statement. He wasn't sure he understood but needed to know more. He was becoming more accustomed to the vibrations their words emitted and was now comfortable standing, clearly viewing the multitude before him.

A new desire for this unknown connection welled up within him, one that exceeded the wants of this world and its mundane existence. Slydin's focus realigned along with his need to accomplish the task set out by Elder Ronne.

"You said, the Source was imparted to you. How does this happen? What does this do?"

The Source will bestow its nature in abundance and where you lack, bring you to wholeness. Then, you will develop to reach the same expression toward Him and all reality around you. After this you will equalize and be created anew.

Slydin was now confused as silence overtook the assembly. They all remained staring at him with their bright, unblinking eyes. Their shimmering, phantom-like bodies obstructed his view of the garden surrounding them. Then, as one, they looked upward. Following their example, Slydin did the same.

How could I not have seen that before!?

Right above his head was a storm cloud twisting into a cyclone. It was huge and covered the area where they stood. As he observed this phenomenon, lightning shot out from its edges and what sounded like a song issued forth from this tornado. Slydin could not make out the words, but while listening, the tempest became more intense. A fiery splendor quickly emanated in a brightness around the circling clouds.

He was overwhelmed and the fire from the storm engulfed all the beings with him. Slydin wanted to shut his eyes and fall to the ground, but instead was held upright by the burning force. This fire consumed and scorched the thoughts in his mind. Slydin's memories and ideas were violently purged from his intellect as it replaced his essence with its own.

It won't stop. Help… someone… who am I?

At once, his awareness was enhanced and he could observe what surrounded him. It was as if the essence of his sight had been transferred into the storm. The limits of his vision expanded and all of reality shifted as his consciousness widened. It became impossible to tell if he even had a body.

Am I floating? Or is the storm expanding?

Colors cascaded just before a sudden shock struck him. It seemed he had collided with the ceiling of existence as a calming presence engulfed his being.

Have I left my body? What am I standing on?

Reality altered and an azure sky stretched out before him. Slydin could still see in every direction at once but there was no horizon. His senses failed to completely adjust to the overwhelmingly impossible display. He felt an ever-widening sorrow created by the uncomfortable pain that gripped hold of his soul, as he failed to navigate this new state of being. Amidst this deficiency, he found that his surrender provided an unstable, yet serene completeness. His senses adapted to this peace, and the parts of himself that were lacking came to surface. Slydin was forced to subdue his fear and allow himself to be healed.

"This is the Source. He restricted Himself to create a physical existence."

Restricted…? thought Slydin. *How is it possible that any of*

Him could ever be restricted?

His vision blurred and he lost all focus. Slydin quickly tried to stall the process. He didn't want to leave the presence. A swift darkness fell over him as he fought against it, trying to retain his state.

"No… Wait! Why can't…"

Slydin's vision adjusted. He was on the hilltop with the garden surrounding him. There was no trace of the gathering. He stood alone once again.

A virtual screen from his wrist indicated the AshScript was speaking for the garden.

"Our friends are calling for you."

"The beings… from this nation. Where are they?" Slydin asked.

"I do not see them."

A clear path opened through the garden. He followed without hesitation, pondering in his heart all that had transpired.

The widespread garden opened a path before Slydin while he journeyed back towards the ship. Unlike his original approach, he carried an imprint of something greater left by his encounter with the beings. His mind filled with a river of questions that flowed so quickly he could barely lay ahold of only one.

After a journey that seemed to take no time at all, Slydin arrived at the ship. Some of the crew eating from the garden vines took notice of him and signaled for the others.

"Captain?"

As he advanced, he raised his hand in response. Julianne rushed out with a confused and angry look, betraying her calm tones. She shielded her face from the sun as she addressed him.

She's pissed. I guess I would be, too.

"Captain Slydin, where have you been?"

"Sorry, I made contact. It was far more intense than we would have expected. But, I think I know what we have to do… what's going on?"

The crew had their hands covering their faces.

Was the sun that bright? Slydin thought as he turned and noticed twilight had begun to set in and the brightness of the day was fading. Perplexed by their behavior he inquired further.

"Is something wrong?"

"Yes Captain," answered Julianne, nearly speechless, "…you're glowing."

What? Glowing? How is this possible? Slydin looked down at his arms and noticed them illuminating. *It's coming from my face.*

Quickly, stroking his head for the light source, it became apparent that it was originating from his forehead.

"Okay… What the hell is this now?!"

"Captain, why don't we go inside the ship?" Julianne insisted.

Entering swiftly, Slydin found his way back to the Captain's chair. He turned facing the bridge. The crew immediately sheltered their eyes. Julianne handed him a helmet. The conversation did not get far before he discarded it and just turned the other way.

"Now that we solved *this* problem, what has been happening in my absence?"

Julianne stared at Mane, urging him to start.

"Sir, we sent out search parties and eventually it was the child of Diklah that informed us that you were… not here."

Thinking about Mane's report he quickly became puzzled.

"So, what did the garden tell you?"

Mane looked almost embarrassed and unsure how to reply.

"Sir," Julianne interrupted, "all of the reports from the AshScript told us you were in heaven."

Makes sense, he thought.

"We searched for days," she said. "We couldn't get a straight answer from the garden or communicate with this planet's beings."

"Days?" Slydin called out disrupting her ranting. "What do you mean? I just left."

Everyone gasped at the comment indicating how truthfully wrong he was. A few moments passed before Julianne could find the words to answer Slydin.

"Captain…" she continued, "you've been gone for just over six weeks."

"Six weeks…?"

It certainly did not feel like much time had passed at all. Was that because I was beyond time itself? Was I mentally there? Or was I actually in that place? I still don't know what that place was.

"Captain," Julianne called out, interrupting his thoughts, "what happened to you?"

Slydin could hardly begin to explain what he had been through.

"To tell you the truth, I do not know how to describe where I was or what happened," he started.

"Through the AshScript we learned you were… in Heaven?" Mane added.

Slydin let the statement roll inside his head. Before replying, he called for a crew member to retrieve a towel from his chambers.

"Heaven? No, that barely covers it. You don't understand, Mane. I wasn't out of my mind or in some altered state. I don't have the words to describe it. What I experienced was more real than reality itself."

Mane went silent and the crew member returned with a towel. Quickly, Slydin wrapped it around his head to cover the harsh glowing emitting from his brow and stood up.

"I may not be able to tell you, but I can show you. We should gather outside."

"Captain," Julianne insisted, "Everything has been so bizarre. Nothing here makes any sense. What will you show us?"

"The Source," Slydin replied. Out of all the words he could use, this was the most truthful and made him sound the least crazy. If that were possible.

"The Source of what?" she probed.

He was stuck for a reply. Slydin was immersed in this for over a month and still couldn't even pull together a sentence to accurately describe his understanding.

"…Everything."

The entire bridge emptied outdoors as the sunset was in full motion. With light dimming and darkness setting in, all of them sat in a circle with Slydin at the head, his back to the ship.

"Sir," Mane interjected, "we tried to communicate with them several times. We could only talk with the garden. How will we be able to make any sort of contact now?"

Slydin struggled with his question. There was no easy way to explain what needed to be done. In order to interact with these beings, they needed to become like them.

"Mane, listen… Everyone…," he announced calling for the crew's complete attention. "You all need to trust me. I can't order you to do this. If you really want to learn what our mission was about, then follow me."

He didn't have a clue how to start, but he knew gathering his friends together had some effect. Slydin unwrapped the towel from his head. The sun had almost set and the surrounding darkness was dispelled by an intense brilliance radiating from Slydin's forehead. Many of the crew instantly shielded their faces. Before beginning, Slydin gave them time to adjust.

"This is it. We are going to complete our mission. Everything we have done has led us here. I don't have any idea how this will work, but I do know that we have to do this together."

The crew nodded in silent agreement and then sat quietly. They waited as the sky dimmed, further increasing the brightness which was now enhanced by the surrounding darkness. At first, the crew stared at their Captain, then looked at one another. The swaying of the garden could be heard as a gentle breeze swept through the area.

Now what? We're all here. What do we do now...? Slydin deliberated as the setting sun finally brought calm.

As if in answer to that question, the AshScript had swarmed through the background without anyone noticing and swiftly swept through the ranks. Each crew member was assailed as a single letter sealed itself onto their foreheads. The experience was painful. The letters gave off a red glow, burning their way into their skin. Slydin, observing the situation, become aware that his illumination soothed this condition.

"Everyone closer to me, now!" he ordered.

The crew dragged themselves to him.

"Take your hands off your faces!"

Some of them had to be forced by Julianne to comply. It didn't take long for them to realize what was happening. As Slydin's light made contact with them, the burning red AshScript became a cool blue, and an easeful stillness soothed its way into their midst.

The crew now had a glowing like Slydin, but not quite as strong. Some of them rubbed their foreheads out of fascination, while others smiled at the relief they now felt.

Before anyone could relax, Crimron drew the crew's attention toward what Slydin could already sense. Surrounding them now, were the beings he had encountered before. This time there was no fear or painful consequences.

"Be at peace. You have arrived to complete a great work."

The crew remained composed. They looked at one another and then to their Captain, who had little idea of what to do next.

"What work are you talking about?" Julianne suddenly asked.

"You have arrived to complete the work of Creation and ascend to match the perfection of our Source. Without this perfection, the universe and your home will fall into complete ruin."

"Okay, so, what is this perfection?" She continued, "How do we achieve this?"

"Perfection is invisible. We can only know light from darkness. This is the work you've been called to complete."

Julianne was now completely confused. "If we can't see it, then how do we know what it is?"

"Perfection is the correction of our defects. All of our flaws were made to exist so we would seek their complete repair. This repair allows us to know perfection completely."

"Why haven't you spoken like this with us before?" Mane added. "The last time we tried to do this, we were barely able to function."

"You could not stand in the presence of The Source before today. Through the words, you and your friends are one

complete soul. In order to stand before the Source, you must achieve at least the first degree of perfection. You can only do this together."

"What does it take to become you?" Julianne enquired, interrupting Slydin's feeble attempt at formulating any sort of coherent requests.

My whole crew was thirsting for this, Slydin deliberated. *Why don't I have the same desire?*

"To become this way is to evolve into a single soul-unity. With every spark added, the fire grows, consuming and transforming all matter into itself. This collective evolution allows for a true participation and perception of reality."

Slydin fell into a reflective comprehension of what they were saying. The crew meditated deeply on the answers these beings provided. Everyone could feel their influence course through them. It was like the AshScript, but far more profound. The effects of an altruistic gravity pulled them all into itself, subjecting their nature to its own. Slydin felt the change happening within them, a change he resisted at first, but the choice was clear. He was ready to take a leap of faith and contribute to the repair of the universe.

"If you are all such *enlightened creatures*," Crimron asserted, "then why make us come all this way? Our home is being destroyed. If you are connected to this… source, then why didn't you come for us?"

"Even with infinity within us, we have been restricted to this world. Should we extend too far into the material universe, our presence would bring about an aggressive change. This development cannot come through coercion. It must be chosen willingly."

"But how will our change help?" Crimron insisted. "We are so far away and have no means to return. If you are restricted here, then will we be restricted too?"

Despite the deep sense of harmony this gathering produced, Crimron's assertion thrust Slydin out of the state he had risen to. The reality of the situation quickly ruined any hidden hope and forced them all to confront the great deficit that weighed against their mission. For the first time, the influence of the beings was completely suspended and despite their presence, he could no longer feel the Source that operated behind them.

Severed from the force that dominated their existence only moments ago, the beings stood clearly opposite the crew.

"All of existence, since the beginning, has been undergoing great changes to reach this perfected state matching the Source that created us. This is the outcome of life.

Looking up, Slydin noticed there was no azure sky or flaming whirlwind. Just the dark night and the multitude of glowing sentient beings surrounding them. The crew looked to him as one, not sure what to make of their last statements.

"We are made one by the word."

The beings faded as a swarm of AshScript besieged the area. As the light from the beings gave way, the AshScript seemed to steal their glow and completely illuminate the surroundings. The letters circled within the group and glowed in a mixture of red, green and light blue colors. The profuse mix of coloration made it hard to determine what they were seeing. Observing their patterns, Slydin became hypnotized by their fluid shifting as they rounded the space between the crew. The beings were now gone and the AshScript appeared to cover the entire planet.

The crew remained completely entranced by the letters. The rising sun imbued the AshScript with a bright gold. The script was immersed and then, by its light, dispelled entirely. Slydin noticed, a seal over the foreheads of his comrades, similar to his own.

Now, we are equal.

None of the crew knew what to do, but despite their very real inadequacies, a powerful harmony extended through their awareness, forcing them to adapt and evolve to a new rhythm of life.

Everyone still had the marks on their foreheads. Since last night they could instinctively speak with the garden and no longer needed the AshScript. The presence that accompanied the beings could still be felt, albeit in a lesser form. Many of the crew members were immersed in a conversation with the garden. They just stood there staring at it using their newly acquired sense. Julianne approached Slydin.

"No one has any appetite," she stated. "The garden says that from now on, we will not need to eat. That this food is set aside as an inheritance for others."

He looked at her, not sure what that meant, but also not disturbed by it. Slydin and his crew now unanimously operated under some sort of internal direction that dictated its will over them, transforming their nature. The concept of eating had become foreign and in the days, that followed the gathering, it was revealed that even becoming tired, angry or feeling any sort of bodily or emotional pain was now virtually absent from their disposition.

Most of them took little comfort in long discussion. Just managing this sixth sense overwhelmed the need for anything else. It attuned them to a greater inner vision that allowed the perception of the world in its entirety. Everybody saw past a cosmos of forces and into a universe of souls.

Entering the ship, Slydin found Mane hard at work. His seal slightly illuminated the virtual screens he had open before him. Silently, he moved onto the bridge, but due to their shared oneness, Mane became instantly aware of his proximity.

"Captain, it's almost finished!" he stated.

Looking over his shoulder, Slydin realized he was reconfiguring some of the hardware.

"I have rerouted the port gate and calculated the location of the Federation. We should be able to open a portal that leads home without a problem," added Mane.

"Really?! I thought it would be too far for us to pass through? How is this possible?"

He pulled away from his desk and looked up at Slydin. His seal still glowing and his face almost saddened by the news he was about to deliver.

"No, Captain, not for us. The AshScript. It has been imbued with the attributes of bestowal. It knows this planet, us and the beings who aided us. This new AshScript is the message we will send to the Federation."

Only Mane would have figured something like this out. Even with the profound connection between us, there is still so much I want to know, mused Slydin, regretful of his previous negativity towards him. "What message are we sending to the Federation?"

"We're telling them to come home," answered Mane. "Want to step out and see?"

They both exited the ship and witnessed the hexadic gate rising from the ship's framework. The crew had amalgamated around to observe Mane's latest development. After the gate finished emerging, Mane gave a countdown and it started up. An upright flowing pond contained within the gate materialized indicating the portal was active.

"Now," Mane began, "the AshScript is completely self-sufficient. It will spread through the portal and after the launch, find its way to the worlds we came from."

"How will it know where to go?" asked Crimron.

"Our knowledge is now part of the AshScript. The letters allow for perfect communication without any intermediary. This is our instruction and it will aid the Federation in finding the way here."

A deluge of AshScript flowed in from the surrounding area. It appeared like a swarm of locusts streaming up the body of the ship and into the portal. They moved with such speed it looked as if a fractured shadow had cast around the crew. The surge lasted for what felt like hours, eventually casting a shadow over the entire land. And then, it was gone.

Mane turned to Slydin and extended his arm. "Captain, it has been an honor serving you. I would never have believed such a gift could ever exist and for me, would never have been an option, if I had not been recruited with you. Thank you, Captain."

Slydin shook his hand gratefully. "Mane, you have always proven your worth. I could never have gotten this far without you. Tell me though, what will it be like when we arrive?"

Mane thought calmly for a moment. "I am not sure. But I know it will be amazing when we all get there."

A bright, golden flash stunned his vision as a single AshScript letter quickly followed the others into the portal. Slydin smiled slightly and upon looking back, Mane had vanished.

At first, Slydin felt a rush of sadness, but not long after, he detected Mane's presence. He was on another plane of existence, aiding his friends from there. The rest of the crew stood shocked at the phenomenon. Shortly after, they all grouped closely together and began to walk along the edge of the garden perimeter. Juliane paired close to Slydin.

"Captain, what happens now?" she asked.

"Now, we move to another level of being. It's a whole other life. I can barely explain it because there is no explanation. It simply is," he informed her.

The garden's instinct could not be nullified and it continually offered food for them. Many of the crew members stopped to thank their vegetal friend. In that instant, their bodies became immaterial and their seals took off for the portal.

"Do you think we will ever be able to go back there?" Crimron asked his Captain. "I honestly thought we would be going back home. I need to see my family again."

"Crimron, this place is home now. There is no going back. We've carried everything with us and now, it's up to your family to make it here," he said assuring him.

Crimron smiled brightly and while slightly laughing, said. "I know. I think I've always known."

Another golden letter slid towards the portal. Now, only Slydin and Julianne remained in a tangible form.

"You think we should have made more efforts to stay in Ripath?" he joked. "You know, I would never have expected this. Even now with all the awareness, it hardly seems real."

She looked over, laughing, as they smiled at each other.

"Why do I follow you everywhere?" Julianne asked, slightly distressed by the unknown she was about to move into.

Slydin remained quiet for a short while, remembering their past as children and feeling the breeze that swayed through the green canopy surrounding them.

"You were the reason I was able to keep stable these last years. Without you, *this* would never have happened. You were the one leading me."

She hugged Slydin tightly. Crying, but also smiling.

"You did well you know. You really kept it together," she said. Stepping away she looked towards the ship. "See you on the other side… Don't wait too long…"

A golden flare filled his vision and Slydin was alone. The beings of pure intellect returned a moment later. This time, there was no thunderous voice storms or fiery visions. One being from the multitude came forward and the two talked as friends.

"When we began our work, we attempted to perfect all of physical reality. But not all of it was ready. Thanks to your efforts, that is now possible."

The two continued to walk the perimeter of the garden.

"Wouldn't this have happened anyway? All life is controlled by the Upper Force, so how can we have any bearing on this world?"

"Our power comes from free choice. It would happen by a cooperative instruction or in its own time. You and your crew have sped up the process and prevented great sufferings throughout the universe," the being responded.

"Why me? Why not someone more intuitive, like Elder Ronne?"

"The development of your elders was intrinsic to their nature. They had no way of passing on this quality to the other nations. The purpose of creating our system this way was so we could function independently and pass this to others. The system acts a ladder that we can climb back up to the Source. We find the Creator clothed in the fabric of reality. Each one of us is set within the system to draw down revelations of the unperceivable Source to bring light into the darkness of this world. The garments that clothe reality are being pulled back.

Slydin contemplated what he said and felt the time in his form come to an end. Staring upwards, he saw a bright azure firmament spread out before him.

"This planet. I never asked its name."

The being faced him with the same shining eyes and stoic look and responded as he drifted from sight.

"Earth."

"How fitting."

The golden seal left his body. Slydin was almost tempted to chase it down, but resisted. He did not want to miss anything during the transition. His thoughts turned to his fallen friends, his crew, family, the Elders and his time at the academy. As Slydin faded from the material, he saw past the firmament to white shores and then a country of green under a swift sunrise.

We have set the keys and called out to the nations of the Federation to shed their burdens, take up the word and return to The Source of all life.

"Counselor Jandin, we still haven't been able to ascertain the reason for all of this."

Jandin turned, leaned on his cane, halting his exit from the council chambers. "Reason? We have established this is an ancient technology turned loose on the public. It was confirmed that the AshScript was developed in Bavel. Due to the secretive nature of the Bavelim, few really understand its inner workings, making turning it off quite difficult for us now."

"Counsellor, the nations have ceased all conflict. We cannot deny that the Federation has never been at peace like this. Even after the defeat of the rebels there was no…"

"Enough!" Jandin interrupted. "Do you hear yourself? We have clear evidence that Edom was hunting for this technology. That means that *he* probably planned for this. I will not allow segments of the Federation to go on some collective pilgrimage to some non-existent location across the universe. We keep the jump gates off and the borders closed."

"Counselor, please. I beg you to investigate further. The

effects of the AshScript have provided a remarkable break-through in negotiations and the planet it talks about definite-ly exists. Please, reconsider."

Jandin shifted his weight off his cane and continued his exit.

All of this work to reunite the Federation. We have no Elders. No Ambassadors. No academy. Our new hierarchy has provided safety and provision for every race and nation. After so much sacrifice and everyone wants to abandon their homes. It makes no sense. This has to be the bane of Edom; some sick joke.

The AshScript flooded the nations of the Federation, repeating the same phrase. Despite causing a unity among the populace, the letters could not be dispelled and have ceaselessly swarmed the nations, filling people's minds with information about higher worlds and evolution. Yet, every-one who deeply engaged in contact with them had about as much information about their source as they did before all this happened.

Go forth from your birthplace to a land that I will show you.

Jandin lay on his bed. He noticed the AshScript swarming on his ceiling.

"You guys don't give up. But you're a technology like any other. When we find a way to turn you off, all of this will pass and we will get on with our lives."

Jandin did enjoy some of the benefits from the invasion of AshScript. The empathic awareness gave him and his coun-selors a greater connection to their peoples and allowed for successful negotiations with rebel nations to remain unified with the new Federation. The bizarre physical manifestations that plagued several worlds had also subsided. But this message wasn't going away and it was influencing the populace.

He turned his head away from the ceiling to get comfortable. Along the wall, a small line of AshScript lined his vision.

"You again, eh? Might not want to waste your time. I'm going nowhere."

He stared at the lettering and noticed a strange shifting. He could not read the script, but in his mind's eye, he observed what it was saying.

The ship was not destroyed for nothing.

That's new. *Ship?*
…
…

He took a sudden breath in as a realization hit him. He struggled to reaffirm his hold on a distant memory… he recalled a fleeting moment from the past.

…Slydin.

ABOUT THE AUTHORS

Vito Andrews is a former professional magician who writes with the enthusiasm of a hyper-active puppy.

Author of "the funniest emails I receive at work," Vito has a joyful outlook on life that's augmented with the endless pursuit of deep contemplation. He lives in Ottawa with his very patient wife, beautiful son and jerkface jerk of a cat.

Matti Silver is the creative, right side of the brain among his friends.

His forte is intricate world-building and the shooting down of logical, sound ideas. While the rest of the world makes 1-screen indie retro games, Matti releases an MMO that has its own language so every nationality is equally burdened by it. A lover of film, comic books, fantasy and anime, he takes it upon himself to combine all the best ideas and present them to the world, like a master curator of fine taste and limitless free time.

Besides his endless energy and eclectic taste in everything, Matti loves nothing more than reading everything except speed limit signs and expiry dates on his government documents.

If you enjoyed reading this, we would love it if you could leave a review. Reviews are the lifeblood of our authors and allow them to keep producing quality content.

Thanks again for reading and make sure to check out www.evwpress.com for more works from the publisher